"Any preference for an engagement ring?"

The yellow diamond he'd thought of had no place here. There was no sunshine in this room. She was locked in a permanent winter. "I was thinking Ceylonese sapphire. It has the same unreachable blue of your eyes."

"I need nothing but a signature on the marriage license. This isn't a time for celebration," Lise responded.

"I understand. But what do you want?"

Rafe couldn't mistake the glitter of tears from a woman who, by their agreement, was denying herself everything she'd desired.

"A convenient marriage, nothing more."

He nodded.

"Thank you, Rafe." The words were breathy and heartfelt. As he looked at her, he saw the princess she'd been, before her tone hardened and she became his queen once more. "My private secretary will be in touch."

"I'll await his call." He stood and bowed. The move was stiff and unfamiliar.

Rafe strode out of the study, his footsteps echoing down the marbled halls. He might have agreed to marry Lise, but he refused to honor the rest. He had time now. This was a battle he would win. He'd marry, then execute a fresh plan.

A plan to win his wife.

Behind the Palace Doors...

The secret life of royals!

Heavy is the head that wears the crown. It's a truth that Princess Lise, Duke Lance and King Alessandro know all too well... Whilst they might spend their days welcoming the world's diplomats and their nights at exclusive balls, that doesn't mean their lives are as picture-perfect as their royal images. Could having someone to share that responsibility with change *everything*?

To claim her crown, queen-to-be Lise must wed. The man she has to turn to is Rafe, the self-made billionaire who once made her believe in love. He'll have to make her believe in it again for passion to be part of their future...

Read on in
The Marriage That Made Her Queen
Available now!

Look out for
Lance and Sara's story
and
Sandro and Victoria's story
Coming soon!

Kali Anthony

—

THE MARRIAGE THAT MADE HER QUEEN

HARLEQUIN
PRESENTS

If you purchased this book without a cover you should be aware
that this book is stolen property. It was reported as "unsold and
destroyed" to the publisher, and neither the author nor the
publisher has received any payment for this "stripped book."

Recycling programs
for this product may
not exist in your area.

ISBN-13: 978-1-335-58384-0

The Marriage That Made Her Queen

Copyright © 2022 by Kali Anthony

All rights reserved. No part of this book may be used or reproduced in
any manner whatsoever without written permission except in the case of
brief quotations embodied in critical articles and reviews.

This is a work of fiction. Names, characters, places and incidents
are either the product of the author's imagination or are used fictitiously.
Any resemblance to actual persons, living or dead, businesses,
companies, events or locales is entirely coincidental.

For questions and comments about the quality of this book,
please contact us at CustomerService@Harlequin.com.

Harlequin Enterprises ULC
22 Adelaide St. West, 41st Floor
Toronto, Ontario M5H 4E3, Canada
www.Harlequin.com

Printed in U.S.A.

When **Kali Anthony** read her first romance novel at fourteen, she realized a few truths: there can never be too many happy endings, and one day she would write them herself. After marrying her own tall, dark and handsome hero in a perfect friends-to-lovers romance, Kali took the plunge and penned her first story. Writing has been a love affair ever since. If she isn't battling her cat for access to the keyboard, you can find Kali playing dress-up in vintage clothes, gardening or bushwhacking with her husband and three children in the rain forests of South East Queensland.

Books by Kali Anthony

Harlequin Presents

Revelations of His Runaway Bride
Bound as His Business-Deal Bride
Off-Limits to the Crown Prince
Snowbound in His Billion-Dollar Bed

Visit the Author Profile page
at Harlequin.com for more titles.

To my amazing children, who called me an author before I'd published a thing. You are my favorite cheer squad xxx

CHAPTER ONE

'YOUR MAJESTY, I'M PROFOUNDLY sorry for your loss.'

The words scraped as if fingernails scoring down a blackboard documenting Lise's short and, up until recently, inconsequential life. She splayed her hands on the ancient mahogany desktop, strewn with newspapers all screaming headlines like, *Ready to Rule?* Challenging the reality that even if she wasn't, there was no choice. As she sat behind her father's desk in a study that had been the seat of her family's power for six centuries, those headlines taunted her.

Imposter, they whispered.

Lise took a long, slow breath. Trying to ease the twist of fear choking her since that awful moment thirteen days earlier when the King's private secretary, Albert, delivered the world-ending news.

'Your Majesty, there has been a terrible accident.'

Now, she repeated the silent mantra she'd chanted daily. A reminder of who she was in those terrified times since. *I am Annalise Marie Beten-*

court. Her Most Serene and Ethereal Majesty, Defender of the Realm.

Soon to be crowned Queen.

The youngest Lauritanian monarch in three hundred years.

Fraud.

She moved her gaze to the man sitting in the chair opposite her. One who didn't appear as *profoundly sorry* as his words implied. His dark eyes glinted, almost as if he were hungry. A shiver chased down her spine and she pulled her jacket tighter against the midnight caress of desire, the remnants of which still haunted her. Once, this man had made her feel the centre of his *everything.* How she'd lapped up his interest like a kitten at a forbidden pail of cream. Basked in his attention, his flirtation.

It had all fed the gluttonous delusion that she had choices in life. Whispered words intoxicating as a drug, which had led her to believe that she truly meant something to him. Rafe De Villiers. Businessman. Billionaire. Devastatingly handsome with a shade of stubble grazing his angular jawline. Looking dissolute. Disreputable.

Unsuitable.

Yet how she'd hungered for those moments with him, basking in the delusion that this brilliant, charismatic man wanted *her.* Igniting a need burning away common sense, which in other circumstances should have warned her that those seemingly clandestine meetings they'd engaged in whenever he visited the palace couldn't have happened by mere chance. They *must* have been orchestrated by her father.

'Thank you, Mr De Villiers.'

They'd been on a first-name basis once. She'd thought she love— *No.* It had all been an illusion, and there was *nothing* to thank him for. Seeing him now, lounging opposite her dressed in a three-piece suit of elegantly rumpled grey linen as if he had not a care in the world, she was once more assaulted by the gut-wrenching truth. The one that had been forced home in that last, most catastrophic argument with her family... She meant *nothing* to him but a means of accessing power in a blighted deceit concocted by her father and Rafe. One where she'd been halfway fooled into believing they might marry for love.

The humiliation of it all seared like acid in her gut. One more wound to add to the growing list of them inflicted upon her over the past few weeks. It was a wonder she hadn't bled out. Death by a thousand cruel cuts.

Yet she was still standing. Barely.

Rafe pulled up the sleeve of his suit and glanced at his watch, then settled his wolf-brown eyes on her again. She raised an eyebrow. Tried for imperious, although she wasn't sure it worked.

'Am I keeping you from something?'

The corner of his mouth quirked, tugging at the pout of his lower lip. Months ago, she'd been fascinated by that mouth. How she'd craved his lips on hers. Twenty-two and never been kissed. Now she'd missed the chance. Lise blinked away her moment of fancy. Those immature, naïve dreams. She could never forget he remained a schemer. Devastatingly handsome, tempting as Lucifer, but a schemer, nonetheless.

'I have all day for you, ma'am.' His voice was dark and sweet as treacle. So tempting once, to lose herself in every syllable he uttered. 'I was only wondering when—'

A rap at the door interrupted him. It cracked open.

'Ah,' he said, raking a hand through the overlong curls of his black hair. An unruly strand fell artfully across his forehead. Everything he did appeared artful. A study in masculine magnificence. 'Morning coffee has arrived as expected.'

She'd forgotten how well he knew the rituals of the monarch's schedule, whilst she was still learning its dictates. Lise glanced at the carriage clock marking out the interminable hours on the King's desk. The desk that should have been her brother's when the time came, rather than this unnatural sequence of events.

When in his office, at half past ten precisely His

Majesty had stopped for coffee. No one ever asked whether *Her* Majesty wanted to do the same. They *assumed*, the pace of change here glacial at best in an institution that had endured virtually unchanged since the thirteen hundreds.

A black-uniformed, white-gloved woman wheeled in a trolley laden with petite delicacies, a royally embossed silver coffee pot, and eggshell-fine cups. She poured Rafe's beverage without asking how he took it. Reminding Lise that he'd spent a great deal of time here with her father, the King, making decisions about lives they'd had no right to make. Such as hers.

Rafe took a mouthful of coffee, tipped back his head, and groaned. That sound of almost carnal pleasure rippled through her, heating her coldest inner reaches.

'I'd have sold my soul for that coffee. Hadn't slept in twenty-four hours when I received your summons...ma'am.'

She tried not to think of what might have kept him up all night, leaving him rakishly dishevelled. In the overcharged atmosphere of gossip-filled ballrooms, rumours flitted amongst the women about his prodigious...talents. Her cheeks burned. She gritted her teeth, loathing how he still affected her.

When had this obsession of hers begun? The plan to trap her hatched? At her coming-out ball?

The day she'd been told she wasn't allowed to compete in the downhill skiing championships. That instead she was going to finishing school as if she were some poorly made-up object, requiring honing to be *enough*. She'd barely held it together that night, feeling small and wounded at a party she no longer wanted because it was celebrating her imprisonment and not her freedom. Until she'd looked up at the interminable roll of guests parading down the wide marble staircase into the glittering ballroom, and there had stood Rafe. Brooding over the crowd as if he'd owned it. All dark unruly hair, a fascinating contrast to his perfectly tailored tuxedo. Wild, untamed beneath the civilised veneer.

Then he'd turned prescient black eyes onto her, and everything had melted away. The pain, the crushing sense that she'd be trapped for ever. And he'd smiled, not taking his eyes from her as he'd descended that staircase in the palace ballroom.

Had he seen it then, the naked, hungry hope on her face? The wish that someone would value her for who *she* was rather than the institution she represented? Because no one had cared what she wanted…

His approaches to her after that night had been respectful, careful. With subtle flirting in the brief moments when they'd crossed paths at official functions. Then she'd turned twenty-two.

And the attention that had been fleeting had become focussed. Private. The soft words and gentle touches. She'd felt beautiful, *desired*. Like a woman with needs and wants that might finally be satisfied.

More fool her at how deep the betrayal went. But as tempting as it was to immerse herself in the humiliation of it all, she didn't have time to drown. Lise wiped damp palms over her black skirt, the uniform of mourning. Seventy-seven days of it remained, but she would never be free, even though the official grieving period might end.

Her family were consigned to the grave because of her.

'You never complained about His Majesty's summonses,' she said, trying for magisterial. Sounding waspish instead.

'I'm not complaining about yours.' Rafe hesitated, then took another sip from the embossed porcelain, which seemed absurdly delicate in his strong, capable hands. His eyes lingered on the newspapers. Pictures of the horse-drawn funeral cortège. Her walking behind, head bowed. 'Whatever business you have with me can wait. You're allowed to grieve.'

His voice was low, seemingly kind if she could have trusted his intentions as honourable. But to grieve? She wished she could rage, scream, cry… but her recent life had been like wading through snowdrifts, blindfolded. The paralysing inertia of disbelief threatening to freeze her solid.

'The Constitution waits for no one,' she said.

'You're the first Queen in—'

'One hundred and fifty years.'

She didn't need reminding. Her parliament, and particularly Prime Minister Hasselbeck, did that daily. Almost from the moment her family's crypt had been closed. Not only about her obligations, but her shortcomings…

'The country's waited over a century for the rarity that's you. They can wait a while longer.'

Rare, precious, beautiful. She'd heard those tempting words slip from his lips before. Shiny sentiments that had called to her covetous soul. The one that had craved to be loved, until she was shown how tarnished the empty words truly were. She refused to listen now. They held all the value of fool's gold when the truth was inescapable. Her country didn't want her but had no option but to keep her.

Lise took a trembling breath and tried to rein in her emotions. Sadly, being the spare not the heir, and a female at that, meant her lessons had all been designed to turn her into a beautiful, biddable bargaining chip. No preparation at all for her current predicament. Assessment of her beauty she left to higher powers. The gossip rags extolled all kinds of physical virtues; a sporty figure, blonde hair and blue eyes…

Being a bargaining chip was a given for most female members of the aristocracy in her frustratingly backward country. Useful to forge alliances, seal deals with auspicious marriages. But biddable?

No. If she had been, her parents and brother would be alive today.

'Time's my enemy.' And it had run out. A wedding had been arranged for the Crown Prince long before he'd died. The prime minister thought it expedient to keep the date and the arrangements for her own wedding. The invitees would have been much the same, anyhow. All she needed was a groom. She swallowed down the sick, dark ache. The taunting voice inside and its insidious whisper, *I can't.*

She ignored it. Her duty must be done. No matter how little she wanted what must come next, she couldn't allow her country to be plunged into uncertainty over succession. Not like this, not unplanned. For that, she needed Rafe. Because everyone who learned about the history and constitution of their small, landlocked Alpine country knew that for her to take the throne there was one, simple requirement.

For a Lauritanian queen to rule, she must have a husband.

When she had been nothing more than a pawn in whatever fresh political game they played with no chance of sitting in the seat she now occupied, Rafe was the man her father had chosen. After months of him circling, those meetings she'd at first believed were chance then kidded herself meant something far more, the truth had been revealed in that final, terrible argument with her family. When she'd been *ordered* to marry him.

She'd refused. Refused to follow her family on their yearly break, where she knew intolerable pressure would be put to bear. The King, the Queen and the Crown Prince ignoring that she was a flesh-and-blood woman, not merely Lauritania's Princess. A woman with hopes and dreams of falling in love, who'd wanted desperately to believe she'd meant something to the man in front of her.

It was her deepest shame that because of her refusal, her family had died.

Lise didn't miss the brutal irony the universe cast her way. For now, Rafe was the only choice. Her duty. Her penance.

Rafe had to know what was coming. Yet here they were, toying with one another. She could hardly bear to ask the question of him. But she had her own plans. Her punishment for cutting off her family's lives. Her brother would never get to marry his fiancée or rule the country he was born to. Her parents would never see grandchildren, the future for the throne they'd so craved. She was required to atone for what she'd done.

She'd marry the man her father had chosen for her.

Lise stood. So he stood. Damned protocol. She kept forgetting and ended up with people bouncing about like a jack-in-the-box. She must remember she didn't move for people now, people moved for her. And Rafe moved so well. Nothing unnecessary about him. All long, lean muscle that his clothes only accentuated. Everything he did, calculated and perfect. *Calculated*…one word she must never forget. That was what she needed to become.

'Sit, Mr De Villiers.' He took his time doing so. Rafe obeyed no one. In a place built on protocol and stricture, he carved his own path. Which was why she'd been shocked when her father had told her the deal he'd secured, with a man who no one told what to do. Not even the King.

Lise walked to the mullioned windows, staring over the towering peaks of the Alps. Swifts wheeled and soared on the air currents, so blindingly free the jealousy twisted her heart. She wished she could join them. Catch a thermal and fly away. But she was landlocked here as everyone else.

'I require a husband.'

'You don't *want* a husband.' She didn't miss the acid in his tone. When he'd tried to see her after the argument with her family, she'd refused to give him an audience, even though her father had demanded it. 'Change the Constitution.'

She clenched her hands into fists, her nails cutting into her palms. 'That's been tried and failed.'

'In 1863 and 1974. Times change.'

Not in Lauritania. Her country was conservative to the core. Even worse, her people didn't trust her, as the headlines in those infernal newspapers attested. The child conceived as an insurance policy in case the worst happened, with no expectation that it ever would. She was the country's consolation prize. Second best. Unwanted. As Rafe knew too well. She'd poured out those childish hurts when she'd trusted him. How cruel of him to presume she now had a choice. 'You know why you've been asked here. Stop pretending otherwise.'

'I think you need to spell it out for me. I'd never presume to know a lady's mind, *ma'am*.'

The formality of him. Lise whipped around, turning her back on the view. She used to love the way he appeared to savour her name on his lips. *Lise.* Like water to a parched man. All lies. She got right to it. There was no prettying the truth.

'I'm asking you to be my husband.' The words

almost choked her. Lise glimpsed the mercenary gleam in his eyes. A gleam she'd mistaken for desire, once. Her own foolish mistake.

Rafe steepled his fingers. 'You want me?' His voice was a low murmur, gentle as a caress. Once she'd been desperate to believe anything his alluring timbre promised. That being forced to give up the sport she loved, the freedom she sought, didn't mean her existence was meaningless. But deep in her heart, it had been more. Her own secret craving that, in a duplicitous world surrounded by simpering imitations, this glorious man might love *her*.

But conceding the point was a fatal weakness, even though a whisper of heat flashed over her cheeks. She straightened her spine with all the hauteur she could muster. Later, she'd allow herself to crumble but not today and never in front of him.

'I'm carrying out my father's last wish.'

Rafe's lip curled into the beginnings of what looked like a sneer. 'A fitting tribute for a great man.'

Another shiver skittered down her spine. Or not so great if the rumours she was now hearing were to be believed. She was coming to suspect her family were only human, even though they had pretended otherwise. Sadly, she'd always been held to a higher standard by them.

'I'm pleased you see it my way,' she said. This was payment for what she'd done. And she would pay, for the rest of her life. But she had a few tricks up her coal-black sleeve. She might do a deal with the devil, but she wasn't in the business of selling her soul completely. She waited for Rafe to settle back into his seat, to acquire the look of smug self-satisfaction that had become all too familiar in her life, before she pounced.

'Have you heard of a *mariage blanc*, Mr De Villiers?'

Rafe swallowed down the gall rising in this throat. He'd flown through the night, cutting short a business trip to answer her summons. Sure of what it meant, what he had been waiting for. Now this. *Mariage blanc.* A white marriage. A marriage unconsummated.

'Yes, I've heard of it,' he said, keeping his voice deliberately bland.

'Excellent, that's settled.' Lise sat down once more, her hands twisting restlessly on the desktop, looking decidedly *unsettled*.

'What's settled?' He leaned back in his seat again, trying not to hiss the words through gritted teeth. Indolence was a look he'd perfected over the years. If he appeared not to care, no one could touch him. The aristocracy here had tried, since school, to destroy the upstart farm boy he'd been marked as. No matter that his family had a wealth of their own, although born of hard, physical work rather than lofty inheritance. When his brother, Carl, had died, they'd almost succeeded in crushing him. But he was made of stronger stuff than any of them realised.

Lise frowned. 'Our marriage, of course.'

He sat back, nibbled on some innocuous sweet thing from the plate before him. Took another sip of his now cooling coffee. He never wished to be seen as the pretender, a choice compelled rather than freely made. That would *never* satisfy him. He'd spelled it out to her father, emphatically. The only way he'd marry Lise was if she said yes, without compulsion.

He gave what he hoped was his most neutral look, when all he wanted to do was bare his teeth and snarl. 'What does a so-called *white marriage* have to do with that?'

Her plush lips thinned into a pale, tight line. 'It's what I'm offering.'

Madness. This was not how things were supposed to be.

He'd asked her father for six months to win her. Never doubting it would take him fewer to secure the hand and heart of this woman who he'd wanted to come to him willingly. So she'd believe he'd been her choice alone. He'd been disdained enough for his working-class background.

He would not have anyone say the only way Lauritania's Princess would marry him was if she was forced to do so. No. He'd wanted to show them all. Their Princess had *chosen* the commoner above the aristocracy.

Yet what had happened? He'd been called away on a brief business trip a couple of months into the job and her father had pounced. Trying to force Lise into the marriage. A woman who required finesse and tender care. Instead of a happy homecoming, he'd returned to a debacle. Lise, refusing to see him at the risk of calling the palace guards when he tried. The King enraged that one of his subjects would dare disobey a direct command— ignore the fact she was supposed to be his precious daughter.

And him? Everything he'd planned, his careful manoeuvres for *years*, in ashes.

He'd wanted to tear the smug portrait of her father from the wall, chop it to matchsticks and hurl it into the closest fire. Then, in a fit of pique on that fateful day which led them here, the King allowed the Queen and Crown Prince to travel with him in one vehicle. Probably to plan how to force Lise to accede to their command. Not to speak of palace security, capitulating to the act of foolishness. All of them grown fat and lazy on complacency. If the mundanity of a rock fall and car accident hadn't killed her family, Rafe feared he'd have been tempted himself.

How many hours had he sat here negotiating? Asking the King to trust that he knew what he was doing. But like all the rest of them, that man could never believe a mere commoner might know better how to manage the Princess than he did. As they'd never believed Lise could ever love him. And now he was picking up the pieces.

Lise sat dwarfed behind a hideous monstrosity of a desk. Skin pale as the permanently snow-capped peaks around them. Dressed in severe black, the dark lace mantilla over her head an ill-fitting crown of grief. She should be in bright, dancing colours. Decked in all the shimmering jewels he could provide. He'd planned from the moment he'd set eyes on her. A triumph to show the blighted aristocracy here what he could achieve. Being loved by royalty. Taking one of theirs as his own. The man they'd underestimated. Dismissed. Her yes to the proposal was meant to be emphatic. Carefully orchestrated, of course, but unequivocal and full of joy on her part. The King in his infinite arrogance had destroyed it all.

'No sex?' He lingered on the word, and her cheeks bloomed to a fetching shade of rose. He still affected her. Good. Rafe suppressed a smile. 'No.'

He had some cards to play here. Lise *needed*

him, for more than one reason. Were things in the country worse than disclosed? Was that why her father had tried to force the marriage prematurely?

Did Lise know?

Her face paled even further if that were possible. Her mouth puckered as she no doubt nibbled the inside of her lower lip. A habit of hers when she worried, and she worried too much.

'What do you mean "*no*"?'

'My meaning's plain.'

'You can't force me to allow you to…' Her gaze darted about the room, never at him. Of course she was nervous of this arrangement. Lise was a woman who sought a fantasy. From the sweeping love stories she read in secret, to the pre-Raphaelite artists she preferred. Each one a homage to the romance she craved.

'Make love to you? I'd never force a woman.'

'There's no love in our arrangement.'

But there could have been. He'd have ensured she loved him when the time came to ask for her hand. From commoner to prince…the aristocracy would never have underestimated him again. The wicked flame alight in his gut burned hotter at the chance lost.

'Have sex, then. No love, merely slick, sweaty—'

'I—I can see you're not interested in a practical arrangement. I'm sorry for wasting your time.'

Lise's chest heaved. The pupils of her luminous blue eyes blown wide and dark. 'I'll find other candidates. Alternatives have been proposed.'

Alternatives? Now who was the fool? He needed to tamp down this anger before he overplayed his hand. He could see them all, jockeying for position to become the most powerful man in the country. Those men who thought they knew better. School peers who'd tormented him at the prestigious Kings' Academy for being of the wrong class, even though his family's wealth crept close to theirs. Disdained his younger brother, Carl, whose only dream had been to tend the family herd on the mountain slopes. Bullied so mercilessly he'd refused to return after six months, when if he'd stayed at the school, he might still be alive today...

Even now, Rafe's wealth propped up the institutions and lifestyle the aristocracy so loved. Every drop of fine wine they drank, much of the food they ate, had the De Villiers name attached. His empire built by his own hands through ambition, driven by personal experience and his brother's blood. Yet none of that mattered. To them, he was still the son of a cow herder, as they'd used to mock him each lonely day at that godforsaken horror of a school. Ignore that for generations his family had made a traditional cheese with its own appellation, national protection and of world renown. That with his own business interests, he could buy them all and still be left with billions. Carl had been right. That place and those boys had taught him nothing but contempt. Then when Carl had died, they had heaped only scorn, not solace, on his grief. He would never forget.

Never.

None of his former collegians, the aristocracy here, had any idea how to save the country, which was why he'd been chosen. He'd show them all what he could achieve. The thought of *any* of them touching Lise raged fire in his gut. There was only ever one candidate for her.

Him.

'I've never pretended to be a eunuch. Yet you're consigning me to the life of one.'

He'd planned it. The ring, a diamond the colour of sunshine to match her golden hair. A wedding night where he'd spread her on the marital bed and show her passion she'd never dreamed of. Nowhere in this scheme was a woman who wouldn't touch him.

'You misunderstand. No sex…with me.' She flushed again. Each emotion playing through the colours washing her cheeks. Her face hid nothing. A charming quality for a lover, a flawed one for a queen. She straightened her spine, tried to meet his gaze but her haunted blue eyes didn't rest on his face. Flitting everywhere about the room, other than on him. 'You can, of course, take a mistress. After an appropriate time.'

Was she serious? The tight set of her jaw told him she was. He swallowed down the bitter taste of her offer as if it were poison.

'What would you consider an appropriate time?' He gripped the arms of his uncomfortable chair till his fingers cramped. Better that than giving into his desire to break something, like the clock on the desk, which wouldn't stop its infernal ticking. 'Should I begin after the honeymoon?'

'We need no honeymoon. It's not that type of marriage.'

'Why wait, then? You'll be wanting a lover too. It wouldn't be fair to deny the goose what you're offering the gander.'

'I am not a goose, Mr De Villiers.' Her hands trembled; she placed her palms flat on the dark, aged desktop again. 'You've said enough.'

No, none of this was enough. The absurdity enraged him. 'I wonder. Shall we invite this…brace of lovers to the wedding?'

'Be. Quiet.' Her lips were tight and thin. He wasn't inclined to listen to the tone of warning in her voice.

'What intriguing dinner conversation we'll all have. Though the question, *Darling, could you please pass the salt?* might lead to confusion. I mean, which darling? The spouse or the paramour? I can see us all grappling over condiments in our efforts to please.'

'There will be no grappling—'

'Not between us, no. Not even a clinch in the corner, sadly. I'm a faithful man, so I'd never cheat on my mistress with my wife. It's against my principles. I presume you'd feel—'

'Enough!' Lise bolted to her feet. Chin held high. Colour florid on her cheeks. Here was the magnificent woman they'd tried to train out of her. 'I'm overjoyed to hear how faithful you profess to be. However, there will be no scuffles over the salt and pepper. No cosy dinners for four. In my experience, kings have mistresses, so you're welcome to your own. All I demand is that you remain discreet.'

Her father had kept a varied group of women who catered to his every whim. Rafe wondered whether she was aware that her mother's private secretary had done far more for the Queen than answer correspondence and post letters. Coming from a family where his parents loved each other in the same blinding fashion as when they first met, he found royalty's convenient arrangements sickening.

But love wasn't for him, the only game he'd played and lost. Learned that the daughters of the aristocracy wanted him for one thing, to irk their parents by flaunting the commoner. He'd always been an exercise in rebellion for those women. Rich enough so as not to be an embarrassment, but never enough on his own. He'd fancied himself smitten with a count's daughter. Till he'd proposed and she'd mocked his audacity. He'd learned then, love was for fools. It had no place in his life, leaving him open to its own brand of ridicule. He would not deign to be scorned again.

Power was a currency he understood. It was *everything*.

Love? It made you powerless.

'What about you, Your Majesty?' Propriety and protocol were the armour she wore, so he'd allow her to hide behind it for a little while longer. Time enough to start stripping her down, piece by tantalising piece, when the wedding ring was firmly on her finger.

'I need a husband. I don't need a lover.'

Her admission that there was no usurper lurking in the wings made the primitive creature curled inside him growl in satisfaction. Still, he played her game, for now.

'That's hardly fair.'

'How generous of you to think so.'

'I'm all for equality where pleasure's concerned. In fact, I ensure my partner's pleasure exceeds mine.'

Her dusky lips parted. He'd never kissed her, something he'd regretted. Perhaps he should have been more assertive in his approach. But he'd thought he'd have all the time in the world to seduce, not to conquer.

'There's nothing equal about a constitution which allows a king to rule in his own right whilst requiring a queen to marry.' Her voice was soft, with a tone of defeat. He loathed the flatness of it. He wanted her to fight for what was hers. 'But it's what I face so I'm doing my duty.'

'And when your duty comes to having an heir and a spare or two?'

'You're referring to children, not objects as the monarchy so often treats them.' She raised her chin and stared him down with eyes as cold and brittle as first winter ice. 'For that reason, there will be none.'

Lise's frigid gaze threw a chill down his spine. She was brutally, bitterly serious. This was not where her hopes and dreams lay. He knew. She'd whispered her secrets to him when they'd seen each other, in carefully planned but seemingly spontaneous meetings. She'd begun to open the door to her deepest desires and now that door slammed in his face.

He stared at her, rigid in the chair opposite. Her eyes fixed on the wall over his shoulder.

'What about succession?'

Lise took in a breath, her body shuddering. 'The monarchy dies with me.'

Rafe reared back, the shock of her pronouncement like the frigid slap of a first winter's gale. No. *Never.* He could not accept this. His children and his family's blood should have been destined to rule the country in perpetuity.

'Lise—'

Her eyes narrowed. 'I haven't invited you to use my name.'

She held herself as aloof as any royal he'd ever met. He loathed that she was directing this charade towards him.

'Since you invited marriage, I believe we're past honorifics.'

'Only when I say so, and you haven't agreed to my offer.' Her skin blanched so pale it appeared translucent. The shadows under her eyes stood out, dark and bruised. 'There are two choices, Mr De Villiers. Yes, or no.'

No meant she would be lost to him for ever. Yes, and by a quirk of the constitution he'd be in a cold and empty marriage, but he'd be King.

King.

He could never forget those who'd sneered at him, laughed at his heritage, bullied Carl from school leaving him in harm's way, mocked his brother even in death. Thought he was beneath them because of his business interests rather than being born into the aristocracy. He'd have power over them all. His blood ran thick and hot at the lure of that thought.

'Yes. I'd be honoured.'

Lise's shoulders softened for the briefest of moments before her spine filled with steel. 'The prime minister suggests a sensible date is a month away.'

On the day the Crown Prince had been due to marry. The horror that her government could do this to her. Why did she allow it?

'How convenient.'

'It is.' He couldn't miss the hard edge of anger in her voice then. 'Rather than wasting money and effort on planning another event. The coronation will occur immediately after.'

This country couldn't even give her a day of her own. Proof that they had never seen her as an individual. He clenched his jaw. Perhaps he could offer her something for herself.

'Any preference for an engagement ring?' The yellow diamond he'd thought of had no place here. There was no sunshine in this room. She was locked in a permanent winter. 'I was thinking Ceylonese sapphire. The same, unreachable blue of your eyes.'

She hesitated for a heartbeat then shook her head. 'I need nothing but a signature on the marriage licence. This isn't a time for celebration.'

'I understand. But what do you *want*?'

He couldn't mistake the glitter of tears from a woman who by their agreement was denying herself everything she'd desired.

'A convenient marriage, nothing more.'

He nodded. Unable to say another word lest anger overtake him.

'Thank you, Rafe.' The words were breathy and heartfelt. As he looked at her, he saw the Princess she'd been, before her tone hardened and she became his Queen once more. 'My private secretary will be in touch.'

'I'll await his call.' He stood and bowed. The move stiff and unfamiliar.

Rafe strode out of the study, his footsteps echoing down the marbled halls. He might have agreed to marry Lise, but he refused to honour the rest. He had time now. This was a battle he would win. He'd marry, then execute a fresh plan.

A plan to win his wife.

CHAPTER TWO

LISE STOOD IN her chambers, surrounded by a small group of women. Her hair, curled into an elegant chignon. Her make-up, perfect. A few ladies straightened the skirt of her wedding dress, adjusted the veil then stood back to admire their handiwork. She shut them all out, refusing to look at herself in the long mirror, as they twittered that she should.

Long ago she'd dreamt of this day. With her mother here, helping her dress. Soothing her nerves…although the Queen had never been particularly motherly or soothing, in Lise's dreams her parents could be anything she desired. It was what she'd secretly longed for. Love, not cool formality. Devotion, not duty. A time when she envisaged a future full of joy, love and hope.

She doubted that there would be any joy in this place ever again.

'We're done here. Please leave me.'

The group bowed and drifted from the room, taking their excited chatter with them. A familiar burn stung her eyes. The make-up artist had applied waterproof mascara, so there was no risk of the hours of hard work being ruined by errant tears, which she'd only ever cry to herself.

Alone.

Her father had said, on the only time he'd confided anything to her, that being monarch was a solitary job. She understood that now. She'd refused even a bridesmaid today. The natural choice would have been Sara, her brother's fiancée. Her only real friend. Two young women, battling the palace in their own way. But how could she parade Sara down the aisle on the day Sara was meant to be married herself? With the press salivating over any signs of her friend's grief? It was too much. Lise wouldn't do it.

Anyhow, this was a job she needed to perform without support. Sure, someone was walking her down the aisle. The prime minister took that starring role. Fitting that he should give her away, having previously dismissed her and her desires, just as her family had.

It didn't matter now, anyhow. She smoothed trembling hands over the bead-encrusted satin of her dress. A gown Lauritanian seamstresses had worked day and night to complete on time. Her dress the *one* thing about this wedding she'd had any choice in, and even then, the designer had tried to change her mind. But she wouldn't be swayed. There was nothing to celebrate.

Today was meant to be endured.

A knock sounded at the door. Time to go already? She swallowed the bitter taint rising in her throat and stilled her quivering fingers. 'Come in.'

The door opened and Albert Thomsen, her private secretary, entered the room dressed in an impeccable dark suit. She wanted to run and fling herself into his arms because if anyone in this place had given her guidance and counsel over the years, it was him.

But queens didn't run or fling themselves about. So she waited where she was, for him to come to her. He bowed.

'The prime minister's on his way.'

'Thank you, Albert.' He was a person more like a father than her real father had ever been. A man who'd held his job since the King took the throne. He remained a solid, stable presence since taking over the role as her secretary, easing her into the job. Helping her around any missteps. Praising her minor successes.

People, like the prime minister, had counselled that it was time for Albert to retire. They'd suggested replacement cronies no doubt. But Albert wanted to continue with her, and Lise had no intention of losing her only other friend in this place.

'You make a beautiful bride, ma'am.'

Her heartbeat raised a few notches at the thought of her upcoming wedding. Rafe, all six feet two inches of lean muscle and brooding presence, soon to be hers. It was as if a bird had trapped itself behind her ribs. She pressed her palm to her chest and took a few slow breaths.

He'd never be hers. He was a means to her end.

'I'm not sure the designer agrees.'

'If only it were a happier day for you.' Albert clasped his hands behind his back. Looked at her in that enigmatic way of his that told her nothing but made her question everything. 'It's a courageous choice, ma'am.'

She laughed, a bitter, sharp sound with no amusement in it. There'd been nothing courageous about anything she'd done. Lise nibbled the inside of her mouth.

'You used to call me Lise, once...'

Albert had always been there for her. Providing gentle advice and encouragement. Warm, where her parents' approbation had been a cold wedge.

'That's before you became my Queen.'

'And Annalise, when you were angry at me.'

'Have I ever been angry at you, ma'am? I can't recall,' he said, though his mouth twitched in an almost smile.

'When I took the crown before father's state function.' She'd wanted to try on those precious jewels. Back then, the certainty was they'd be her brother's some day. Never hers. All the diamonds and gold and ermine too much temptation for a teenager. She'd stolen into her father's rooms where it had sat in an ornate wooden travelling box. She'd discovered the crown was big, and heavy. That was when she'd dropped it…

Albert chuckled, his elegant grey moustache quivering. 'No one noticed the mark, and the Crown jeweller repaired it.'

That was a secret they'd kept from the King, for everyone's good, Albert had said at the time. She'd believed people were keeping secrets about her meetings with Rafe once. For whose good was that?

The telltale burn started behind her eyes once more. Would it ever stop? She tried to blink away the tears. Queens did not cry. Of that she was sure.

'What do you need, ma'am?' Albert's voice was warm and kind. Almost her undoing.

'I need to be just Lise, for a little while. Please.'

She glanced at the view from her private rooms. She'd always loved the vista from here. High on a hill above the capital, Morenberg, surrounded by the Alps she loved. The mountains where she felt truly at home. But today they loomed outside, as if judging her.

'You'll always be Lise to me. Even though I call you Your Majesty.'

She turned to him, still standing there, a picture of gravity and stoicism.

'I don't think I can do this.'

'You were born to it.'

'No one taught me the skills.' Nobody thought about her much at all. Her brother was meant to take the throne and she was meant to do her duty, which she'd failed. Spectacularly. What if she'd simply agreed to marry Rafe when her father demanded it? She'd have been wedded off the same as now, and the rest of her family would be alive.

'Some need to learn, and some have it here.' Albert tapped the centre of his chest. 'You've always cared about your people, Lise. No one needed to teach you that. Your instinct will carry you through any mistakes. The rest? I'm here to help.'

'Which I never doubted.'

His lips tilted in a sad smile.

'Have as much faith in yourself as you have in me and you'll do well. Is there anything else you need?'

A way to escape? But there was none. The die had been cast weeks ago. Still, Lise gritted her teeth. She'd wanted to wait till after the official mourning period was over. Three months, that was all she'd asked for. Only a small delay. But no, her government had been clear.

You must secure the Crown.

The silence between them hung all too knowingly in the room. The clock chimed the hour. Dread curdled sick in her stomach.

'Almost time to go,' she said, itching to adjust her veil as the pins fixing it pricked into her scalp.

'I think I need a few moments to myself before the prime minister arrives.'

Albert gave her a curt, well-practised bow and turned.

'Albert?' He stopped at the door as she said his name.

'Yes, ma'am?'

Her moment of being *just Lise* was clearly over. 'What do you think of my decision to marry Mr De Villiers?'

As she'd barrelled from the room after the final argument with her father, Albert had been there. Directly outside. There was no way he couldn't have heard everything she'd said, but his face had told her nothing as she'd run down the halls to her own apartments, her world torn apart.

Albert smiled. 'I've always thought you were a woman of great courage, Your Majesty.'

Rafe stood at the altar of the Morenburg Cathedral. The whispers of the assembled crowd echoed from the vaulted ceiling, melding into an amorphous hiss. Rainbow colours from the centuries-old leadlight stained patterns on the floor like blood spilled on the marble.

He stared down the long red-carpeted aisle to the firmly shut front doors. The scent of the lilies bedecking the hallowed space too cloying. He wondered whether the funerary choice of flower had been Lise's, or whether they too had been pre-ordained. Ordered for her brother's nuptials. The probability they had been galled him. That this day, *his* triumph, was recycled from others. He shook his head. No time to think of that since it was only minutes till the bride arrived. Mere hours till he would be King. The most powerful man in the country.

His pulse quickened, the thrum of excitement coursing through him. In the front seats sat his mother and father. Eyes not quite so wide as they'd been over the past weeks since he'd told them he and Lise would marry. For all the ceremony, his parents remained the humble, unaffected people they'd always been. Now, they'd take their rightful places in society, like him. Their grandchildren would one day sit on the throne. The De Villiers name linked to the Crown in perpetuity. His only wish was that Carl could be by his side, to witness his triumph. The pain of that loss knifed deep; a wound barely healed after all these years.

'You sure about this?'

His best man and best friend stood surveying the pomp in the nonchalant way the finest aristocracy could breed. He'd met Lance at school, his father the British ambassador to Lauritania. An outsider, like Rafe. It hadn't mattered that Lance Astill would inherit a duchy in England when his father died. He wasn't Lauritanian, so he wasn't good enough. Apart, they'd been bullied. Together, they'd been impenetrable. Lance had guided Rafe through the raw pain of Carl's death, becoming like the brother he'd lost. The friendship had lasted when Lance's father was posted elsewhere. It had never wavered.

'Yes.' Rafe's certainty was absolute, unassailable. Coursing through his blood with the enthralling hum of a drug.

'I've a car parked round the corner and this.' Lance reached into his inner suit pocket and pulled out the hint of a silver flask. 'Whisky. Plus a case in the back seat. We can make a dash for it through the door of the sanctuary. Escape. Drown our sorrows for days.'

His mouth quirked in the signature lopsided grin that drove women wild. But his eyes were tight and serious.

'No,' Rafe said.

'You used to be more talkative. She's got you cowed already? No stag night. Now passing up decent whisky. Wives, why would you have one?' Lance gave an exaggerated sigh.

An organ piped hymnal tunes, which echoed from the vaulted ceiling.

'Some things are more important than the whisky.' Rafe's words were almost sacrilege. Once it was always about the whisky and the women. But he hadn't needed to celebrate his last night of freedom. This marriage gave him keys to every door. 'Do you have the rings?'

Lance began an increasingly exaggerated farce of patting of his various pockets, frowning. A lesser man might have been worried. Rafe knew it was only for show.

'I believe I do. Somewhere… Ah.' He reached into his trouser pocket and pulled out two glinting circles of gold. 'Hers is spectacular.'

Lance twisted it in his fingers, eyeing off the workmanship. If nothing else, Rafe's friend had a keen eye for beautiful things.

'Her Majesty refused an engagement ring. The occasion dictated something more than a plain band.' The day required symbols. His great-grandmother's wedding ring, tying Lise to him. The family's past coffers reportedly plundered to have the magnificent token of love made, reflecting his great-grandfather's adoration for his betrothed. A waste in his view. Rafe hadn't wanted to accept it when it was suggested by his parents, given the heirloom was the symbol of a devotion absent in this marriage. However, he couldn't turn down the honour of using it today.

'Must be love,' Lance drawled.

Rafe snorted. Not for him. He'd never allow himself that vulnerability. All 'love' had done for him was turn him into a fool. Never again would he dance to the beat of another woman's drum.

'Careful, my friend,' Rafe said, with a smile meant for the cameras directed towards them. 'The world is watching.'

He stared down the assembled crowd. Dour, serious-looking people. All the uniforms, medals and emblems they hid behind as if it made them better than the rest. In a short while he'd be set above them all, and there was nothing they would be able to do but bow and scrape before him. The victory would taste so sweet.

Lance glanced up at the cameras assembled to beam the marriage to millions. 'Nervous?'

Rafe shook his head and spoke the unassailable truth. 'I'm where I should be.'

'But is the bride?'

Rafe checked his watch. She was only five minutes late. Not long in the scheme of things. But the curl of tension twisted his gut. He'd wanted no hesitation. No sign that being at his side was other than where she was meant to be. He shook it off. What did it matter when he had a lifetime as Lauritania's King ahead of him?

'I've been meaning to ask, what is that hideous thing on your chest?' Lance pointed to a pale blue and white ribbon. An enamelled, gem-encrusted star with insignia pinned to Rafe's jacket. 'Looks like a vulture.'

'Order of the Raven.'

The country's highest civilian order in the

country. Since Rafe didn't have a drop of blue blood in his veins, the decision had been made to confer him with something. For outstanding service to business. He could have laughed. He'd been serving the country for years and it took his marrying their Queen to recognise him.

'You're becoming one of them.'

There was the dull sound of disappointment in his friend's voice. It had been the boyhood promise they'd made after Rafe had saved Lance from a beating meted out by the sons of some counts or other. *Never* become like the aristocracy here. From that day, Rafe had fought back with fists, carrying the pride of his working-class background. Together he and Lance had become a force none of the other boys had been able to reckon with.

'I'll never be one of them.' He fixed his friend with a heated glare. 'I'm better.'

Lance shook his head. 'Always the ambition with you.'

The truth of that cut closer to the bone than it ought. 'If that's how you feel, what are you doing here?'

'Ensuring my oldest friend's making the right decision.' The silence between them lingered ominously for a few beats. Then Lance clapped his hand on Rafe's shoulder, lowering his voice in a conspiratorial way. 'And women. The best man always gets laid at weddings. It's a rule.'

Rafe laughed; the tension broken in the way Lance knew best until the organ swelled in a glorious crescendo as the doors of the Morenberg Cathedral cracked open. Trumpets commenced some suitably wedding-like heraldry. The whispers of the crowd drowned out by the music announcing the arrival of his soon-to-be wife. He turned; his bride stood silhouetted in the door. His heart quickened its pace to racing speed.

Lance chuckled. 'My friend, it looks like you're royally screwed.'

Rafe didn't understand what he meant. Lise crossed the threshold of the cathedral doorway, a shadow backlit by glorious sunlight. The voluminous skirt of her dress filling the entryway, nipping tight at her slender waist. She began her slow procession down the aisle, the prime minister at her arm. But as she walked closer, he realised what Lance had seen the moment she'd stood in the doorway. When she'd walked into the soft light of the cathedral nave she hadn't moved out of the shadows. Her wedding dress was an inky black.

He ground his teeth. The perfectly fitted morning suit too tight, too hot under the stage lights. Of all the humiliations in his life he'd had none worse than this. He wanted to tear off the badge of chivalry she'd bestowed on him only days before, the meaningless trinket that it was. Symbols? She'd given him one of her own. Not even a pretence that this was a day to be celebrated in any way. What she wore was an utter repudiation.

Rafe breathed slowly and reminded himself that the world watched every expression they displayed. As his bride approached, he smiled. Wide, doting and fake to the very core. He glanced over at his parents, who were beaming as if her slight meant nothing.

'You look beautiful,' he said. Her face was pale and soft focus behind the black lace-edged veil that fell past her fingertips, spilling to the floor and trailing behind her. And to any objective observer, she did. The gown's bodice fitted to accentuate her slender frame, the elegant swell of her breasts. All the harshness of the colour softened by a feminine ruffle of dark, sheer fabric round her neck that dipped in a demure vee exposing a bare hint of cleavage. The coal-dark satin of the remainder of the gown shimmering with encrustations of jet beading. Up close it was an extraordinary piece of workmanship. It didn't stop the beat of anger drumming in his veins.

The archbishop took his place in front of them as the music died. 'Are we ready?'

He'd spent his whole life planning for a moment like this. Four years manoeuvring for this exact day. Yet it was Lise, not him, who gave a curt nod to commence the ceremony that would seal their future together.

The archbishop intoned a prayer and began. 'We have come together today to witness the marriage...'

With that sentence the hallowed space melted away. The talk of love, joy, tenderness. Of children. Those words should have been a mockery, but somehow weren't. Even the anger burning through him mellowed. Rafe turned to Lise and took her hand in his, as he'd been instructed he should. The tremble in her frigid fingers unmistakeable. Her blue eyes wide and brimming with barely contained tears. And the moment ceased to be about a country, a queen or a king. It centred on the two people in front of the altar, a man and a woman. The vows passed in a blur of false promises. Rafe placed the wedding ring on Lise's slender finger. Her skin soft and delicate as she gently slid the bright gold band on his own with no hesitation.

'... I therefore proclaim that they are husband and wife.'

Rafe raised Lise's veil, uncovering a face as pale as if she'd been cast in moonlight. Her perfect mouth a soft dusky pink. He gazed into the blue eyes searching his face. Pupils wide and dark. The barest blush sweeping across her cheeks before fading away. He raised his left hand to cup her face, which tilted up to him. Her skin, silky and warm under his fingertips, her lips parted. For the briefest of seconds, he believed she wanted this. Him. Then the look passed.

'For pity's sake, kiss the bride,' Lance murmured.

Not today. Their first, real kiss would be in private, not watched by millions. He wanted her to crave it, *beg* for it. For *him*. So he dropped his head and brushed his lips across the smooth skin of her cheek. Relishing her soft exhale as he did.

Rafe turned to the assembled crowd. The coronation came next but that was a mere formality. He didn't need to feel the heavy weight of the consort's crown on his head to know the unassailable truth. It hummed through his blood with a heady roar. Better than making his first billion. Better than drinking the whole case of whisky Lance had stashed in the back of the car outside. For every slight these people had given him, each one of them would know.

The country was his. He ruled them all.

Long live the King.

CHAPTER THREE

LISE TOYED AT the plate of food at the wedding banquet showcasing Lauritania's delicacies, a headache burgeoning at her temple. Other people seemed to be enjoying themselves. Wine flowed freely. There was a sense of festivity she didn't feel. Three hundred or so palace intimates and foreign dignitaries celebrating a marriage she didn't want. A wedding arranged for her brother, not her.

Rafe didn't have any trouble eating as he finished whatever meal lay on his plate. But then, he had what *he* wanted, what her father had promised him. No wonder he could eat, drink and be merry with the rest of them. She brushed away a stray hair that had fallen from her chignon, trying to ignore the sensation of him sitting so close. Gone was the laid-back nonchalance that was Rafe's signature. Today he vibrated, as if filled with some dark energy. In exquisitely tailored morning dress with a silk tie. His over-long hair cut to a more respectable length, but still swept back from his face in that carelessly messy way as if run through by restless hands. Her fingers had itched to touch those glossy black locks as she'd waited for the kiss in the cathedral. The one that never came. Her first and last opportunity. She'd thought for a fleeting moment that today she could steal something for herself. But life wasn't like that, not for her. As she'd gazed into his velvet brown eyes, transfixed by the full curve of his lower lips that would claim hers, he'd turned and kissed her cheek. She would never get to know whether his lips were cool or warm, soft or hard. Whether he was passionate or restrained.

She should have been relieved. A kiss wasn't part of their agreement, even though a kiss was expected, today of *all* days. If he *had* kissed her, it wouldn't really have broken any promises. Now she'd lost her only chance. Though she shouldn't be thinking of chances or kisses. All she hoped was for the day to be over quickly, so that she could return to her rooms, rid herself of her finery. Grieve this sham of a marriage. And steel herself for the next three days allocated as a pretence of a honeymoon, so the country could believe the lie that this was a love match. To give her people some hope built from the tragedy of the past months. And how could she argue against that? Against any of it when she was the cause of the grief? So she was being bundled up and packed off to some unknown destination where there would be more togetherness than she wished to contemplate. Lise's cheeks heated and she took a sip of her wine.

'Your dress is magnificent, Your Majesty.' The prime minister's wife smiled at her. It didn't meet the woman's eyes. No one's smile did. Not even Rafe's when he'd greeted her at the altar and told her she looked beautiful. 'The colour is a brave choice.'

Brave... Why could no one say what they *really* meant?

Rafe stilled next to her, put down his knife and fork. Took a swig of his wine.

Minutes prior to the wedding, a press release had identified the designer as one of Lauritania's finest couturiers. It told the story of the gown with the royal crest and Lauritania's native flora embroidered in beads and crystals on the skirt. So much encrustation that the gown weighed on her, heavy and oppressive, as if she carried the whole country with her.

'It was a way of honouring my family since I'm in official mourning.' The stab of pain above her eye made her wince. She rubbed the aching spot in her temple.

The prime minister's wife brushed her fingers over her jacket sleeve of lemon-coloured silk. Such a cheery shade, which spoke of celebration. It made a mockery of her family's deaths.

'But it's your wedding.' The woman rambled

on. 'Surely on today of all days you're allowed to be a little…brighter. After all, you hope to be a bride only once.'

Lise glanced to another table at Sara Conrad. Her brother's fiancée. She was wearing black too. How would Sara feel, watching Lise marry today? Being crowned Queen in her place? The guilt gnawed at her, bile rising to her throat. Lise couldn't celebrate knowing she'd stolen her friend's future. How could she flaunt her marriage when Sara and her brother had lost the chance of theirs?

She clenched her fists in her lap, her wedding ring on one hand and coronation ring on the other, biting into her flesh.

Rafe leaned forwards. 'Are your parents still alive, Mrs Hasselbeck?' His warm hand slid over hers. Squeezed in silent support. The tight band in her head eased a fraction.

The prime minister's wife straightened in her chair, her mouth pinched and tight. 'They are, Mr De Villiers.'

The cut was so plain it couldn't have been a mistake. A few people stopped eating. An uneasy, expectant silence fell over the table.

Rafe's eyes hardened to stone. Face stern, un-compromising.

'Pardon?' He raised one dark eyebrow in a

supercilious way. Perfectly regal. Her father wouldn't have done better.

'My apologies, Your Majesty.' Mrs Hasselbeck patted her lips with her white damask napkin, nothing at all apologetic in her demeanour. 'It's all so new, I forgot.'

Lise didn't believe the lie for a minute. How dared the woman? Dismissing Rafe was like dismissing the monarchy itself. Lise opened her mouth to say something, but Rafe cut across her, voice cold as steel.

'You should have your memory checked. The lapse is troubling. It could mean something serious for the future.'

Those words spoke a clear warning. That Rafe wouldn't forget or forgive. Lise shivered. This was a side to the man he'd never shown her before. The ruthless businessman, who would do whatever he wanted because he now could.

The woman dropped her gaze, a conciliatory gesture of sorts. 'It won't happen again.'

'That's pleasing to hear,' he said. The moment passed. The palpable tension settling. People turned away from them and went back to their food and wine. 'But my message is that with the advantage of having both parents alive you shouldn't presume to tell anyone who's recently lost theirs how to mourn.'

A bright kernel of warmth lit Lise's insides,

the words a surprise. She shouldn't have enjoyed them. He didn't really care. Rafe simply knew how to play the game of intrigue too well. She couldn't let her silly heart buy into the fantasy it meant something more. He was experienced, she was an amateur, and she must never forget.

Whatever she might have hoped for, he would never love her. In her relatively brief years on this planet, she'd come to realise no one really did. Her birth had been deemed a necessity born of duty. She'd not been truly wanted and, whilst the King, Queen and Crown Prince had seemed to do much as they'd pleased, she had been required to do what she was told. And even when she'd done that, it had never been enough.

The soft strains of a string quartet began, announcing the bridal waltz. Lise let out a slow breath, let her shoulders slump. The ache in her temples hadn't gone. She fixed a false smile on her face. Stared out at the crowd.

Lise dreaded this moment. Rafe stood and held out his hand. She placed hers in his. The warmth of it engulfed her own chilled fingers. He stared at her with his dark eyes, almost black in the room aglow for the wedding luncheon. Her pulse whipped to superhuman speed. Her head pounded to the same thready, anxious rhythm as he led her to the dance floor. She needn't worry, she knew the movements of the waltz. Had suffered through lessons given at her finishing school, when for months all they had seemed to learn was deportment and dancing. She placed one hand lightly on Rafe's upper arm, the superfine wool of his coat cool and soft under her fingers. The muscles underneath hard and uncompromising. He slid his arm round her back, till his palm sat strong and hot below her shoulder blade. Drawing her to him.

'Relax,' he murmured, his voice gentle and enticing. How could she? The space between them too close. She tried concentrating on the elegant knot of his silver tie. The perfect double-breasted waistcoat of pale grey silk. The way the clothes moulded over his strong chest. She looked up at his face, his gaze intent. His all too fascinating lips curved in a half-smile. She could do this, dance with him. Though her breaths seemed short and sharp as if there weren't enough air in the room. All she needed was to let the man lead. Yet the thought of letting Rafe lead… She had no idea where he'd take her. But the slow, curling slide in her belly took her head to places she didn't want to go. Revisiting the fantasies she'd once had of being held in his arms, made love to, adored.

He moved, his powerful legs brushing her dress. Carrying her with him. They rose and fell in time with the music, in perfect unity. The warmth radiating from his body seeping into her frozen one. A prickle of awareness singing over her skin. She could smell him, fresh and crisp like the Alpine forests mingled with something darker, a primal thing that sang to every nerve in her body. That made her want to fall into him, soak it into the frigid heart of her. Yet she couldn't do that, have him draw her close. Rest her tired and aching head on his chest and take some of his strength. She'd made the decision. The lives of her family had been stolen as a result of her actions. She'd devote herself to the Crown. Preparing her country for a time when the monarchy was no longer required. Nothing else mattered. For tonight she needed to straighten her wedding tiara and get on with it.

More people joined in the dance. The prime minister and his wife. *Sara.* Dancing in the arms of their best man. Looking…happy. Smiling up at Lance whereas the swirling and the sound simply made Lise sick and dizzy. The music too much with the pounding of her head, till the colours blurred and she misstepped.

Rafe steadied her. Stopped. Led her from the floor, drawing her into a quiet corner. Or as quiet as any corner could be with the eyes of three hundred or so people watching them.

'You don't look well.'

'It's nothing.' Heartsick wasn't an illness, was it? 'The waltz has never been my favourite dance with all the spinning. I'm dizzy. It's been a long day.'

Up before dawn to dress, have her hair and

make-up done. Trying to numb the pressure threatening to cleave her in two.

'The formalities are over so we can leave soon. No one will ask questions.' His eyes were molten. All liquid chocolate, luscious and addictive. Rafe reached out and slid another unruly strand from her chignon, tucked it behind her ear. The gentle touch of his fingers sent goosebumps sparkling over her skin. 'Then bed for you.'

'It's only afternoon.'

'Indulge yourself.'

Rafe's voice was low and soothing. She imagined her bed now, the plush coverlet of eiderdown. How she wished she could indulge like a normal woman. Sink into it with him. She took a step back as a tempting heat grew between her legs. She couldn't let this overcome her. That wouldn't be honouring her family. She was vulnerable now. Her head throbbing.

She'd master this.

She *had* to.

'I'd like to leave now.'

Rafe stared down at her. He wouldn't miss the looming tears because he missed nothing. He slipped his arm around her waist in a proprietorial way that made something inside her curl with a treacherous pleasure. Motioned to his best man. The pair shook hands. Lance offered final congratulations. Announcements were made. Everyone in the room stood. The men bowed as Rafe led her out, the women curtsied.

The throbbing in her temple increased to a vicious pounding. She massaged the side of her head.

'Anything wrong?'

Everything, and nothing she had any power over.

'Headache. You're right, I—I need rest,' she said as they walked from the ballroom to their private chambers, acknowledging staff as they passed. Together, yet separate. With each footstep the gulf between them widening. It almost felt like relief, yet at the same time she mourned the loss of him. The emotion a confusing mass inside, congealing in her stomach, making her ill.

They stopped outside the door to her room. She looked up at him. So tall, so imposing it was hard not to swoon. Her heart beat a thready, panicked rhythm.

'You need help with your dress,' he said.

Of course, the buttons. Hundreds of them down the back of the gown. She cursed every single one.

'I'll call for my lady-in-waiting.'

Rafe cocked his head to the side. 'There are certain expectations of what will be happening today between husband and wife. One of those is that I'll help you undress.'

What would it be like to let him? The feel of his

fingers slipping each tiny button through the loop, exposing her spine to the air. Would the act be perfunctory, or would he torture her slowly? His eyes became dark and heavy lidded, a look that told her everything. Sensual torture was what he had on his mind, she was sure. And she couldn't allow it because she was weak. She needed hours of sleep to shore up her defences against him.

'I find I'm tired of people's expectations. I've performed as was expected of me. Now I'm done.'

Rafe's perfect mouth kicked into a knowing smile. As if he *knew* she was avoiding him.

'Then I'll leave you to your afternoon.' He took her right hand, weighed down with her coronation ring, lifted it to his mouth and kissed. His lips warm and gentle on the back of her hand.

She nodded as he stepped back. So stiff, so formal that something about it made her want to scream and scream till her throat was bloody. Then he turned and walked down the marbled hall to his own door, without looking back.

Rafe strode into his rooms. Dismissed the valet imposed upon him by palace protocol. Tore off his tie, cast it onto the bed. Followed with his jacket and waistcoat.

His wedding night, and they were engaging in this ridiculous charade. Lise still intent on shutting him out, even though she wanted him. He could tell by the high colour of her cheeks, her quick breaths. Dilated pupils and languid blinks of her eyes when he stood too close. It was enough to make him rush her, but patience had been his virtue in business, and he needed it here. He always fought to win, and with Lise it would be a siege. Long and slow.

Something about the thought licked at him deep and low. He'd started today when he hadn't kissed her as he knew she'd expected from the disappointment on her face. Their first kiss was never going to be a chaste peck on the lips. He had bigger plans for that, a seduction that would seal her to him body and soul, unlike their emotionless signatures on an official slip of paper. Children, so his legacy would last. He'd go down in history as the first commoner to sit on the throne.

She'd be desperate enough for him in the end. He'd ensure it. He knew Lise's secrets, what she'd craved—freedom, acceptance—and they were even more important to her now, as Queen, than as the lonely Princess in her gilded tower. He could still give her those things.

He'd been working towards that moment ever since he'd glimpsed her at her coming out ball. When he'd been announced and walked down the sweeping marble staircase. She'd stood at the bottom, gazing up at him, a glowing smile on her face. He'd been struck as a visceral craving dug its claws into him when their eyes met. They'd been introduced, he'd bowed. She'd smiled even wider, still the glorious, natural young woman who had all but disappeared now, worn down in the name of duty. She didn't know him then, but she hadn't judged the entry of a man without a title, *a commoner.*

He'd wanted to steal her away, run so that she wouldn't be crushed by the purpose of others. Still, no matter his desire, she'd been about to be packed off to some hellish finishing school. A place that taught women to aspire to nothing more than advantageous marriages, bent on turning her into a beautiful clone. By some miracle she'd survived without losing herself. There had been nothing careful and suppressed about Lise that first night. In a room of pale imitations, she'd stood out as unique. So he'd waited. He had patience. She'd needed to find her place in the world before finding it at his side then in his bed. He knew enough about the machinations of the palace to ensure it happened.

After waiting so long for this day it had taken all his strength to walk away. Not to take her in a mind-numbing kiss.

He took a deep, calming breath. They had three days away from official duties. That meant he had three days to make inroads on the siege for his wife's body and soul. To tease, to tempt. She'd come to him willingly, begging him by the end of it. If he were a betting man, he'd bet on being in Lise's bed inside a fortnight.

Rafe removed his great-grandfather's cufflinks from his shirt and placed them carefully on the gilt dresser. Precious heirlooms that reminded him how far he'd come from the cursed farm boy of his youth. Taking his family company and their working-class wealth and turning it into billions. He poured a glass of the single malt whisky he'd requested and took a slug, enjoying the peaty burn in the back of his throat. Swallowing down the anger, mostly at himself. The irritations he suffered at his current situation were nothing when compared to Lise's recent loss. Even though her mother was renowned as a cold, ambitious woman and her father as licentious and profligate. Then the brother who'd exhibited meagre promise but descended into reckless pleasure-seeking, no doubt following his father's example. Whatever the truth of them and however Lise might delude herself, they were still her family.

He needed to remember she was deep in grief, and he well knew the cost of that emotion. Plus, tonight they were still playing a role, and, as a seemingly caring husband, he should check on his wife.

Rafe picked up the internal palace phone and requested a delivery from the kitchens to the

Queen's room. A peace offering, of sorts. Or perhaps his opening salvo. He walked through his expansive apartments to the door that separated him from Lise. A door for which he now had the key. He smiled.

Let the siege begin.

CHAPTER FOUR

LISE STOOD AT the window, overlooking her city decked with banners and flowers for her wedding and coronation. She winced at the light of the bright autumn day as she downed two painkillers in one gulp of water. She should close the curtains, shut out the sunshine that caused her head to pound, but ever since her family's deaths she couldn't, at the risk of the room closing in on her, leaving her gasping and breathless.

She walked to the bed. Perhaps lying down would help, but on the coverlet lay an exquisite negligee her dressmaker had made as a surprise gift. It taunted her, that fragile piece of wedding-night trousseau. Fine, cream georgette, sheer as cobwebs. Cut in with plunging lace and delicate embroidery. A peignoir lay next to it, designed to allow tantalising glimpses of the wearer. Alluring and seductive. She was used to expensive clothes. Cashmere, silk, the finest of wools. Satin evening gowns requiring a surprising number of foundation garments to hold you in or push you out in all the right places to get them to fit with the perfection envisaged by the designers. But this.

Overtly sensual, like nothing she'd ever placed against her skin.

Lise picked up the corner of the nightgown, light as air. What if she slipped it on for tonight? She could wear things like this to bed, she supposed. But this garment seemed overly decadent. Anyway, she knew that an item like this wasn't meant to be worn to sleep. Goosebumps flourished over her skin. Its purpose was to be viewed through male eyes. Something meant to be appreciated in a sweet burst like fairy floss and then melt away at the first touch.

She dropped the fine fabric, teasing under her fingers. It wasn't for her. It could go the same way as her wedding gown. Taken away to be stored in the royal collection with her mother's clothes and all the other wedding finery before it. Held for posterity to be viewed when she was long dead, and her family relegated to history. It seemed a fitting place to bury it, leaving no trace of the Queen who'd married earlier in the day.

Almost.

Lise twisted at the wedding ring sitting on her finger. It gleamed with the burnish of old gold. She wanted to rip it off but knew she must get used to the constant prickle, since it was there till death. Which was what was engraved on the inner surface, in French. *Jusqu'à la mort.* She shivered. There was something almost macabre about the thought. The finality. Though even she had to admit it was an exquisite piece of jewellery. The wide golden band appeared sectioned, each panel inlaid with delicate, alternating enamelled flowers. Daisies and roses. Impossibly fine workmanship. If circumstances had been different, if she'd been able to believe she'd meant something to Rafe, if they'd loved each other, then this ring would have signified so much. If, if, if. None of those things were relevant to her, to this marriage. She needed to forget the romantic ideals she'd held once before her rude awakening and move on.

All she'd proved to herself was that Rafe didn't love her.

The crack and creak of a rarely opened door disturbed her thoughts. She whipped round, the sudden movement increasing the pounding of her head. Lise put her hand to her temple again as Rafe walked through the freshly opened doorway.

'What the hell are you doing here?'

'Hello to you too, Lise.'

Rafe had changed. Gone was the urbane gentleman from her wedding. Before her stood a man dressed in casual trousers, with shirtsleeves rolled up to show his muscular forearms. The front unbuttoned so she caught glimpses of the dark hair on his chest. All of her tightened, as if she didn't fit her own skin. As if she'd burst out of it as a butterfly splitting from its chrysalis.

She didn't like the feeling. At. All.

'I asked you a question!'

The corner of his lip curled in a mild, indulgent kind of smile.

'Apologies. I thought the answer was obvious. I came to visit my wife. To chat about how she felt the wedding went. The normal intercourse between newly married people.'

He strolled further into the room, looking over everything with an astute, all-seeing gaze. Rafe overpowered the space. His presence bigger than the person, obliterating all else. He stroked a finger gently over the surface of a delicate antique French writing desk. It was as if he were looking for cracks, imperfections. Looking for a way in.

She crossed her arms in a protective move, but she didn't feel protected.

'It was a productive day. I woke up. I dressed. I got married. I was crowned Queen. The end, goodbye.'

'We're far from the end of the day yet.' His voice stroked over her as soft and seductive as the silk negligee on her bed, which Rafe was now looking at with unalloyed fascination. Her cheeks heated.

'It's over for me.' She glanced past his shoulder at the opening to his apartments. Once her brother's, though Ferdinand had vacated them years before. The dust covers only recently removed to accommodate a husband. The shard of pain stabbed to the heart of her, but she ignored it. Lise nodded towards the open space. 'That door's usually kept locked.'

He slid his hand into his trouser pocket, pulled out a key. 'I have this.'

'How did you get it?' She'd requested he be placed in the King's Chambers rather than here. Then he'd be halfway around the palace, well away from her.

'Friends in high places.'

This place was full of traitors. Rafe stood in front of one of the large mullioned windows. She squinted as the pain from all the bright light clawed inside her skull. The tablets she'd taken didn't seem to be working. All she craved was to lie down and sleep away the next seventy-two hours. But no, she had a *honeymoon* to participate in, and nothing about that would ease the pain she suffered.

'I didn't authorise it. Give me that key and scuttle back the way you came.' She waved him out. His smile in response might have been mild as a spring day, but his eyes held all the tempest of a thunderstorm.

'Marriage implies a certain level of...availability.'

Another flush of heat crept to her cheeks. 'You can't just barge in here.'

'I didn't barge. I strolled, with purpose. Next time, I'll knock.'

'There'll be no *next time*.'

'It would be strange if I didn't have access to all areas.'

Lise was about to object, but there was a knock at the proper door of her room. Could no one leave her and her aching head in peace? Lise hated knocks on the door now. She could never forget Albert, ashen-faced, walking through another doorway to deliver her the news…

'Yes!' She might have been a little sharp, but life was sharp. Every day held something designed to cut her. The well-oiled door eased open. One of the servants walked in carrying a tray containing a teapot and cups. She put it down on a small table.

'There's nothing more we require. Thank you,' Rafe said with a glorious smile that made the girl blush as she curtsied and left the room.

He took the embossed silver teapot and poured out a pale golden liquid into two cups. The scent of it fresh and herbal.

'What's this?' She nodded suspiciously at the beverage.

'A family concoction. It can cure anything that ails you, so the legend goes.' He held out a cup to her, took one himself and sat on a couch under the window. She sank into a spindly, straight-backed chair, as far away from him as possible. Rafe took a mouthful of his drink and Lise followed with a tiny sip from her own cup. The brew burst minty and sweet over her tongue; with undertones she couldn't place.

'What's in it?'

'The recipe's a closely guarded secret. My mother knows the blend. She won't give me the ingredients. Is afraid I might commercialise it. Shame. I suspect it would be quite popular.'

'It tastes of things I can't place.' Somewhat medicinal, but pleasant and refreshing. It wasn't the sort of thing she imagined Rafe drinking at all, if rumours of his love of single malt whisky were anything to go by.

'I disliked the stuff as a child. It was forced down my throat every time I sneezed. As an adult, drinking it leaves me nostalgic,' he said, taking a mouthful of his own. For a fleeting moment his gaze seemed distant, the crinkles at the corners of his eyes deepening as if the memory was a happy one. 'My mother sends me a regular supply. To help me sleep when my conscience gets the better of me from making too much money, so she says.'

'How's that going?' Lise took a large gulp of the beverage. The quicker she finished, the faster she might encourage him to go. 'Or let me guess. You don't have a conscience.'

'I have a large hoard of herbal tea, which is

now in the palace kitchens hopefully being put to good use amongst the staff… And my conscience is clear.' He chuckled, a warm throaty sound that rolled over her bright, hot and sweet, like the drink in her cup.

She dismissed the sensation, difficult though it was not to simply immerse herself in it and forget her own failings. How nice it would be not to have a conscience, whereas hers tore her to pieces.

'Pleasant for some.'

Rafe cocked his head. 'What could a twenty-two-year-old woman have on her conscience?'

If only he knew. Those hateful words she'd said a constant reminder of the final conversation with her father.

You can all go to hell. I wouldn't cry if you died…'

But that was her cross to bear. She wouldn't share it with him. 'What thirty-one-year-old man doesn't have something plaguing his?'

'Touché.' He laughed, such a strangely cheerful sound in this space that had no happiness in it. 'But the prickle of conscience suggests regret. That's a wasted emotion. Make your decision, stick to it and accept the consequences.'

If only it were so easy. She'd live a life never accepting the consequences of her decisions. Now, Rafe posed a constant reminder of them.

'So you have no regrets and nothing on your

conscience? You sound more like an automaton than a human. Good for you.'

'I've one regret.' Rafe lounged on the floral chintz couch in his typical fashion. Too masculine for this room although he seemed to take ownership of it all the same. 'A very human one. The regret for not kissing a beautiful woman.'

His rich brown eyes skewered her, and her heart rate kicked up, thready and overwrought. It was a terrifying sensation, as if he could see everything she wanted to remain hidden for ever.

'Nothing important, then.'

'Sometimes there's nothing more important than kissing.'

The air in the room grew thick with possibility. Surely he didn't mean her? They hadn't kissed, but that could be put down to part of their agreement. It must be someone else. Someone worldly. Passionate. A woman he could take up with again after a respectable time. The sort of woman he could fall in love with. Not her. Too young, inexperienced…unwanted. That realisation sliced through her, with something almost like pain. The ache in her head intensifying. She rubbed at her temple again, trying not to think about it.

'What's plaguing you, Lise?'

'Nothing.' Nothing she could tell him about. Nothing that wouldn't condemn her, though she didn't know why his good opinion mattered. All she needed was to get away from him and the way he affected her. The pounding heartbeats, which made her head throb ever harder. 'Except this headache.'

'We'd better not let the staff discover your malady, not today.'

'What do you mean?'

'The clichéd excuse for avoiding a husband's advances. *Not tonight, dear, I have a headache.* On the wedding night too. They'll all be wondering about the antics in this room on what's supposed to be the happiest night of our lives.'

She shrugged. 'Maybe they'll assume we both have a headache because they realise it's not the happiest night for either of us and their supposition will end there.'

'I'm not known for my headaches.'

'I applaud your pain-free status.'

'What few people realise…' Rafe leaned forwards with a conspiratorial whisper, his muscular shoulders pressing at the fine white cotton of his shirt '…is that orgasms are a recognised cure. So a headache shouldn't be an excuse for avoiding sex, but an incentive to have it.'

How that three-letter word, *sex*, slipped from his mouth. Accentuated by his voice, deep and tempting, as if it held a wealth of meaning. Once, all she'd dreamed of was a moment when he might hold her, make love to her… A product of her foolish imagination and naïve, romantic dreams. She'd never held any kind of meaning to him. It was the position he wanted, not her. Lise cast aside those thoughts. Rolled her eyes. 'I can see men all over the globe using that line. And there's nothing more to say on the subject.'

'Headaches, or orgasms?'

'The latter.'

'Shame.' Rafe considered her through steepled fingers. 'The tea hasn't helped?'

She peered down into her cup, at the dregs of liquid there. 'With my headache?'

A few random leaves settled in the bottom of the fine porcelain. If someone could divine her future from them, what would it hold? She suspected nothing good...

'Yes. If it gave you orgasms, I'd be the wealthiest man on the planet rather than the wealthiest in Europe.'

Rafe sat back and threaded his hands behind his head as if he was getting comfortable. As if he had no plans to leave. She needed him to go, so she could spend her wedding night trying to forget who she'd married and *why*.

'*If* you were given the recipe,' she said. 'Which you weren't because your mother doesn't trust you and neither do I.'

That seemed to catch his attention. Rafe stopped lounging and straightened. His eyes narrowed. 'In this place I'm the *one* person you can trust. I wish you'd realise that.'

Once, she might have believed it. Not now. She placed her cup and saucer on a side table and smoothed damp palms on her black trousers.

'A trustworthy man wouldn't have feigned interest in me when all the while the deal for my hand was being sealed as a fait accompli.' Her jaw clenched hard. How it galled her, the things his attention made her believe. 'That charade was cruel.'

He narrowed his gaze, assessing and intent. 'My interest was not feigned.'

But he didn't deny the charade. Lise closed her eyes and pinched the bridge of her nose. Tears burning behind her eyelids.

'I can't do this, not today,' she said. More to herself than anyone else but she hoped he listened since she didn't have the energy to fight him. Not now.

'I'm sorry, I've been trying to lighten the mood and you're suffering. Do you need painkillers?'

She looked up at him and shook her head. 'I've taken some. Nothing's working on this headache and right now I'd do anything to get rid of it.'

Rafe raised one dark, strong eyebrow. 'Anything?'

She shouldn't have said that. Not anything, *al-*

most anything. She pressed back in her chair. The delicate, wooden back crushed into her spine.

Rafe stood. He had a look of predatory intent on his face. Her heart beat faster, which only made her head throb more. Though if she didn't have so much of a headache, she might have been more worried. But her voice seemed paralysed as he walked towards her, every movement languid and slow.

'I understand. It's been a difficult day for you. That's why you have a headache,' he murmured. 'I can help with that.'

He moved behind her. The heat of his proximity was warm against her back. She tried to ignore him standing there, but the feel of his presence trickled down her spine like warm water.

'What are you doing?' She squirmed in her chair, trying to see what he was up to. Rafe stood out of her eye line. Without him to focus on in front of her, the whole room seemed too light and bright once more. She winced and shut her eyes against it. All she craved was a few moments of peace, for the pain to leave her. Physical *and* emotional.

'You're tense. It's clear in the way you hold yourself. If what I do doesn't help, I'll stop. Let me touch you.' Rafe placed his hands on her shoulders. Firm, warm. Solid and, in the strangest of ways, comforting, as if through his touch he could absorb some of what plagued her.

'You're carrying the weight of the country's grief, as well as your own, on your shoulders. For a few moments, let it rest.' He pressed his thumbs either side of her spine and she arched back at the exquisite ache of tight muscles objecting under his forceful fingers. 'Let me know if you want me to stop.'

His voice was a soothing murmur as he dug his thumbs a bit lower. *Oh, there.* Lise stifled a moan. Rafe didn't stop the journey of his strong, intense fingertips circling either side of her upper back, finding trigger points she didn't know she had. Working them under his clever fingers till they melted away. She'd had massages by therapists after her skiing, but it had been nothing like this. The intensity that made her forget everything. The hurt, the day. All she concentrated on was the pressure of his hands on her spine.

'No.' Her voice sounded far away. He lifted his fingers. 'Don't stop.'

He moved his hands towards her neck, the pressure making her soft and pliable. Melting her. She dropped her head forwards, closed her eyes. The relief exquisite as he dug in relentlessly. Rafe ran his thumb over a tight spot.

'Right there,' he said, and she exhaled. She couldn't remember the last time someone had touched her, someone who might care. Certainly not her family. Yet all she could do was soften under his ministrations.

He left her upper back and slid his hands to her neck, a tremor skipping down her spine as he gentled for a moment, stroking his thumbs up and down as if searching. His fingers firmed on a tender spot at the base of her skull. Who moaned? Was it her? Rafe chuckled.

'Does that feel good, Lise?' His voice was all gentle temptation. She couldn't resist listening to the way her name rolled from his tongue. 'If you allow me nothing else, let me give you this.'

'Yes.' Her voice was a bare whisper as he kept working her tight muscles, softening the knots in her neck. He scraped his fingers across her scalp and eased her head back till it leaned against his hard abdomen. She didn't care about anything. The voice of crippling self-doubt fell silent. The sharp edges of her life blurring and softening. As he gentled the stroke of his hands through her hair, she could purr like a cat. And when he rubbed the burn at her temples time lost all meaning. It could have been moments or hours since she'd been sitting here.

'Please.' Her body had melted like wax under a flame. Rafe ran his hands through her hair as if straightening it, then slid one hand round the front of her throat, cupping her jaw. He leaned in, mouth at her ear, his warm breath a gentle caress as she tipped her head back to rest on his shoulder.

'I'll give you anything you want.'

She didn't know what she'd been asking for. For him to stop? For him to keep going? She couldn't say. Her tongue, thick in her mouth. Her nipples tightened under her top. She wanted Rafe to slide his hand down her chest, ease the ache with his talented fingers.

'Anything. You only need to ask for it,' Rafe whispered, each syllable full of dark promise. Every part of her in a dream as his lips traced the soft flesh behind her ear, the barest of brushes, which set her body on fire.

Anything. He'd give her *anything*...except, he couldn't. She opened her eyes, blinking slowly to focus. Her freedom, her family. They were all irrevocably lost. All she could do now was to ensure that what had happened to her would happen to no one else. She stiffened. Rafe could offer her *nothing*.

'I want you to stop now.' Her voice came out as a rasp, raw and pained.

He stopped. Immediately. She hated herself for missing his touch, an empty, bereft sensation. It proved her weak, as she'd known. One touch and she was ready to throw herself into his arms, welcome him to her bed. He stepped in front of her, looking down as solid and immovable as the mountains surrounding the palace. She wished she could take some of that strength for herself but taking anything from him was a vulnerability he could exploit.

'Of course,' he said. 'You're exhausted, and I'm being selfish. What my bride needs is a dark room, a soft pillow, a warm bed and sleep. I'll ask the kitchens to send dinner to you here. I can look after myself.' He brushed his knuckles against her cheek. Damn him and his gentle voice, his understanding. Because she wanted it, craved it. She closed her eyes, as he stroked her skin again. Shutting out the unbearable tenderness in his gaze. 'I hope you're feeling better, Lise.'

She heard the door snick as he left her alone, as she'd asked. But worse than the caring he'd shown. Worse than succumbing so easily to his touch. Worse even than the terrible sense of loss of his hands on her body...

Her infernal headache was gone.

CHAPTER FIVE

IF RAFE COULD have developed a perfect torture, it would have been the exquisite agony of touching his wife with no early prospect of release. All night he'd had dreams of her, dressed in the magnificent sheer negligee that had lain on her bed. How it would hang on her body, showing tantalising shadows of what lay underneath. Those thoughts had morphed into imagining what she wore to bed each night, which meant all he'd been plagued by were visions of her lying naked on pristine white sheets.

Now he was in a car with Lise, driving the winding roads to his ancestral home in the mountains. The delicious smell of her, like wildflowers and rain. Everything about her taunted him in this closed-in space. Her golden hair, which had slipped like cornsilk through his fingers. All the softness of her that he craved to sink into. Her breathy moans. Those intoxicating sounds he could listen to again and again. Dreams of him over her, buried deep inside her body. The way she melted under his fingertips. All pliant. Willing. *Please.*

He had no doubt she'd wanted him last night. He was hard at the thought.

But he ruthlessly crushed those fantasies, for now. These few precious days away were being sold to Lise as shoring up the myth of their relationship for a curious public but the reality, for him, was so much more. Which was why he'd driven here rather than allow them to be chauffeured in a car with a little fluttering flag whilst they sat regally in the rear. Sure, there was security following at a respectful distance exactly the way he'd demanded, much to their protestation, but if there was one thing they'd learn, he always had his way. Lise needed reminding that, apart from being Queen, she was a woman with needs and desires. That she could still indulge in simple pleasures without being overwhelmed by misplaced guilt.

'Are you feeling better today?' he asked. They hadn't had breakfast together. She'd slept late and he hadn't wanted to wake her. But as she'd entered the car he'd seen the dark smudges under her eyes, ever present, which told a story all of its own.

'Yes, thank you.' She glanced at him only briefly, before looking out of the window again. 'Where are we going?'

He'd told her it was a surprise, and the look on his face when he had suggested that she didn't much enjoy surprises. Sure, he could have taken her to his mansion in the fashionable area around Lake Morenberg. The type of grand home any wealthy Lauritanian must own, yet a place where he rarely stayed. Instead, he brought her to where he'd grown up. A simple farmer's cottage on land that his family had owned for generations. If there was any place for simple pleasures in Lise's life, then the cottage was the venue to indulge them.

'The first home I lived in.' The home his great-grandfather built for his great-grandmother. Where his father was born. Where Carl… He tamped down the blunt ache of his brother's loss, an ever-present bruise. Those feelings left him vulnerable. Never again would he let that wound be picked open. 'My grandparents gifted it to my parents on their engagement. It's quiet. I thought you might enjoy a break away from the city.'

Plus, there was the sense of freedom these wild places instilled. He hoped she'd find that freedom again, to be herself.

To let go.

His pulse throbbed at the thought of her in any kind of abandon, not holding back. Body arched in the throes of passion, his possession. He would get that from her. Claim it when offered, keep it all for himself. Lise looked at him then, and he chanced taking his eyes from the road for a moment, only seeing an innocence in her he knew would turn to caution if she'd ever guessed what he was thinking.

'That's…kind of you.'

Not so kind, when having her in his bed was the end game. Breaking the promises she'd deluded herself into believing he'd made when they'd reached their agreement about this marriage. So long as he could convince her that it was all her idea, his plans would succeed. For in this place, there was no escape. The house was small and the space intimate. Perfect for a honeymoon if togetherness was what you were searching for. He wasn't sure she'd thank him when she saw it.

'We have a stop on the way first.'

They passed the turn-off to his home, and drove further, winding through green pastures dotted with the occasional cow, to a copse of trees. He pulled off the road and parked at the gravel verge. The black SUV of Security stopped well back, but he'd made it clear that they weren't to follow them into the forest. More protesting. He'd ignored it. Lise needed to forget about being Queen. He saw these small steps as one way. But of greater importance, and what her security team didn't realise, was that he'd care for her better than they ever could. This was *his* land, *his* home. He'd ruled these mountains, been King here, even before Lauritania's crown had been placed on his head.

Rafe left the car and opened her door. The trepidation on Lise's face was easy to read.

'What are we doing?'

He rounded to the boot and retrieved a small bucket and knife as she watched, chewing on her bottom lip, a slight crease forming between her brows. Looking beautifully perplexed.

'Foraging for mushrooms.' Rafe smiled at her as they walked into the leafy verge. Here he breathed deeply of the cool autumn air tinged with the crisp scent of nature. Time slowed. He could travel all over the world, stay in any of the expansive properties he owned, but only here was home. With Lise by his side, it felt more right than it ever had, the realisation a startling one. 'Have you ever been?'

She shook her head. 'It would have required me to get dirty, and that would never do.'

'No making mud pies as a child, then?'

'Now you're being silly.' But she gave him the tiniest of smiles nonetheless, which he took as a win.

'I'm all for giving you new experiences. Mushroom picking comes first. Mud pies come later.'

Lise laughed, and the glorious ring of it sang through the trees. He hadn't heard that sound since the times they'd strolled the palace gardens together before her family had ruined it all.

He craved to hear her laughter again and again, with him the cause of that happiness.

'There's a stream where Carl and I used to play as children and come home filthy carrying frogs and moss. Be careful or we'll go there next.'

'Who's Carl?'

He'd forgotten himself, mentioning his brother's name. Another revelation, that he could lose himself with her, which was a vulnerability he could never afford. Lise was ignorant of the knowledge and the memory he protected, since the pain of Carl's loss had been wielded as a weapon against him in the past, by those richer and more powerful.

He'd never allow that to happen again. Anyhow, there was no one richer and more powerful in Lauritania than himself. Not any more. But uttering his brother's name had been a slip he never made. The only time Carl was mentioned was in the safe haven of family, or with Lance when they'd drunk too much whisky and were intent on reminiscence.

'Rafe?' She wanted her answer. He wouldn't lie to her, but he couldn't respond so forged ahead a little too fast up an incline, deeper into the shade. It was steeper here and Lise didn't really have the shoes for it, pretty little things made for palace halls, not forest floors. She lost her footing and slipped on the leaf litter. He took her hand and steadied her. The slightest tug and she came into his arms easily. The soft press of her body against his as she splayed her hot palms on his chest.

The gleam in her cornflower-blue eyes as he held her told him she was far from indifferent. He ached at the magical feel of her in his arms. Her breaths high and fast. Pupils dilated. He should kiss her here, under the canopy as the breeze skittered through the ochre leaves above them. But he wanted to be somewhere where they could take things to a natural conclusion. In the forest was not that place. Though with a blanket and a picnic...

He wasn't sure where all these romantic notions sprang from.

Lise slid from his grasp, wiped her palms on her skirt as if trying to wipe the remains of him away. Something small and painful scraped inside him as she did.

'Do you know what we're looking for?' Her question about Carl forgotten in a moment where he knew she was as affected by their proximity as he'd been. And he could smile at the change of subject because what he truly searched for was here. Standing in front of him looking beautiful and uncertain.

'Yes. Ceps.'

He turned and strode further into the shade of the trees as she hurried to keep up with him.

'How do I know they're not going to poison us?'

She had so little faith in him. In anyone, perhaps. He'd work to change that, where he was concerned at least. As for the rest of them? They could wallow in her distrust. No one else was worthy of her anyhow.

'Because I've done this hundreds of times since childhood. You're the one who'll try to pick the poisonous mushrooms. I'll make sure what you choose won't kill us both.'

He scanned the leaf litter round the trees. Glimpsed the telltale signs under a break in the canopy. Rafe walked up to his prize. Slipped out a knife and cut the stalk. It gave him the same innocent thrill it had as a child when he'd found his first edible mushroom. The simplest of pleasures that even he'd forgotten over years of becoming hard and jaded both at his business and with his country.

He held up the mushroom. Lise smiled and it was like the sun breaking in the middle of the forest. Warm, dazzling. He basked in it.

'Now it's your turn,' he said, handing her the knife.

'Where do I find one?'

He showed her. Something about Lise here seemed calmer. The lines of stress etched onto her face had smoothed. A tightness relaxed. He suspected the mountains were her place, too. That she felt it as much as he did.

They hunted in silence. He smiled as he watched her. Intent, looking at the ground. She let out a little cheer.

'This!' She pointed, then brushed some leaves away like uncovering buried treasure.

He walked up to where she stood, peered at her find. Slapped his hand to his chest and groaned. 'You're trying to kill us all.'

Rafe spied the pout on her lips, her disappointment. He laughed. 'I'm joking. It's perfect.'

'Not poisonous?'

'No.'

She punched him in the shoulder but grinned all the same. Looking young and happy for the first time in weeks. 'You're mean.'

'You do the honours.' He nodded to the knife and held out the bucket. 'Then find me some more. We need enough for dinner.'

'Who's cooking?'

'Me.'

She stopped, turned. Looked as if she was seeing him for the first time. 'You cook?'

'How else am I going to eat?'

'I don't know.' She shrugged. 'Restaurants. Private chefs.'

His mother would never have stood for that. She believed her boys needed to learn to feed themselves. He'd fought her attempt to drag him into the kitchen as a teenager, but at least had a few meals in his repertoire.

'You can't live on fine dining. Sometimes you want a home-cooked meal.'

He'd never thought he'd need the ability. Yet as Lise looked at him with big, wide eyes in a way that suggested he was somewhat heroic, that simple skill now seemed vital.

She scuffed her feet on the ground. 'I don't know what that tastes like.'

'Then tonight will be full of new experiences for you.' Her cheeks blushed a fetching shade of pink, leaving him in no doubt what new experiences she had on her mind, and they had nothing to do with food. 'But before then we need a few more mushrooms.'

He watched as she continued her search, all so he could cook her a simple meal. Her smiles as she found what she was looking for were all for him and the happiness for what he'd shown her. And Rafe wasn't sure how he'd make it through dinner when all he craved was dessert.

Lise rubbed her hands against her jeans, not completely removing the dirty smudges left by their picking expedition. Their precious cargo stowed safely on the back seat of Rafe's low-slung sports car, filling the cabin with its earthy smell. There, in that small forest beneath these towering peaks, it was as if she could breathe again. The tight band, a constant round her chest, finally easing. Somehow, it was as if the natural grandeur of the mountains diminished her problems. As if she could almost be happy here. Though how could she be happy when her family were lying cold and dead in a grave?

She stopped looking at the view, instead looking at Rafe as he deftly negotiated the treacherous, winding roads that would soon carry the dairy herds down from the tree line to the winter pastures and barns. His hands were relaxed. Long fingers on the steering wheel. Forearms, strong and bronzed in the sunshine. Arms that had wrapped round to steady her as she'd slipped on the loose leaves. The overheated memory of being cradled, safe. It flooded over her, warming like the autumn sunshine spilling through the windscreen. A delicious, hazy sensation that slid inside and had her shifting in her seat.

Rafe glanced over at her. 'It's been a long drive. We're almost there.'

He'd misinterpreted her discomfort. Which was a good thing. If he knew the real reason, he'd use it against her, of that she was sure.

They rounded a corner, turning into a narrow drive that meandered further uphill. Nestled in a tangle of wildflowers and rambling cottage garden sat a two-storey chalet, with steep shingled roof and Juliet balcony up high. The fresh, white-washed walls and dark timber cross-hatching reminded her of a gingerbread house. Wisps of smoke drifted lazily from a chimney.

'This is lovely,' she said, almost with a sigh. Rafe smiled as he pulled his car around the back to where a building stood. The barn, if she had to guess.

'It's a little crooked and well worn being so old, but this has always been home.'

Rafe tugged their bags from the boot of the car. Lise loved the way the muscles in his arm bunched and flexed as he did. She grabbed the bucket of mushrooms. He walked to a back entry and opened it, guiding her through the mud room into a sunny, country kitchen where she placed the bucket on a bench top.

'How often do you come here?' she asked. The place looked well lived in, the wooden surfaces polished to a shine, no dust anywhere to be seen.

'If I'm not travelling, this is where I try to stay.'

That surprised her. Most of Lauritania's wealthy lived on the lake, or in one of the fashionable skiing areas. This part of the country was only known for summer pastures and farming.

'It's so far from the capital.'

He laughed and the deep, masculine sound rippled through her like an earth tremor. 'I enjoy the solitude. Plus, I've a helipad built out back. If pressed for time I fly.'

Another surprise. It was something about him she should have known, but in all the times they'd been together, they'd only talked about her. How much of himself did Rafe hide?

'You could have flown me here?'

'Of course, but the drive is beautiful, and I thought you'd enjoy it. Next time I'll bring you by helicopter. If you trust me.' Something about the fact he'd again thought of what she might enjoy warmed her insides. She liked him caring, she ached for him to touch her. They were dangers she could not succumb to. Because she didn't trust him. She didn't trust anyone any more, least of all herself...

'Come,' he said, jolting her out of those miserable thoughts. 'I'll take you to your room.'

She followed him through the kitchen and up a wooden staircase, the treads burnished to a low gleam by generations of footsteps. On the top floor, the ceiling sloped with the frame of the house. Rafe dropped his bag outside one door. Toed open another and let her inside.

A fire crackled in the grate of a rough stone fireplace. That, and the sun streaming through the doorway to the tiny balcony she'd seen on the drive towards the house, made the room warm and inviting. Dominating the space stood a magnificent four-poster bed with a comforter of rich burgundy. Plush rugs covered the dark wooden floor. In front of the fireplace sat a deep blue velvet couch she craved to sink into and never leave.

But she realised, looking about her, that the room was undeniably masculine with its solid furniture and bold palette. A man's space. *Rafe's*. She turned, and found him leaning against the door, her bag at his feet.

'I can't take this room. It's yours.' How could she sleep here? In his *bed*. It was too much. Her heartbeat picked up its already hyperactive pace. She needed to distance herself from him, not immerse herself completely.

'It's more comfortable than the second bedroom and has its own en-suite bathroom.' He shrugged. 'I thought you'd appreciate it.'

'I can handle having to walk to the bathroom. If I survived Princess School, I can survive that.'

He raised an eyebrow, and his mouth curved into that warm, slow smile of his that did complicated things to her insides she refused to dwell upon.

'Princess School?'

'Finishing school. It was…' stultifying, depressing, demoralising, '…austere. I shared a room with another girl, and we definitely had to share bathrooms.'

'Strange. I thought it would be palatial quarters, hot chocolate, toasting marshmallows, and plotting to acquire rich husbands.'

'The plotting for husbands was there. Along with lessons in flower arranging, correct placement of cutlery, deportment and how to be the perfect lady. All those kinds of world-saving skills. Exactly what I needed for my job as Queen.'

She gave a laugh, which came out more like a hysterical snort.

'Learning how to be a perfect lady was obviously one lesson you paid most attention to.' He grinned at her.

'Obviously.' Lise laughed harder, but there was no joy there, only disbelief at the absurdity of it all. The futility of those twelve, lonely months. They'd prepared her for precisely nothing. Not her family's death, not her new role leading the country. She laughed till she doubled over, then the laughing morphed into the clutch of grief that clawed her throat, of loss and missed opportunities. That her family never saw any more of her than her value as a bargaining chip. As a wife to someone powerful. It was how her country saw her, too. Only her marriage making her legitimate as Queen.

Lise couldn't stop the tide of pain as it overwhelmed her, threatening to rend her in two. She buried her face in her hands, trying to calm herself. To choke back the sob threatening to break free.

She didn't hear Rafe's steps across the floor. His strong arms wrapped round her again, bringing her to his chest. Holding her so she wouldn't break apart. She buried her face in the hard muscle. Forcing down the tears that she'd never allow to fall in front of him. Trapping the sadness with shuddering breaths. Because Lauritania relied on her to pull the country from its grief. She didn't have time for her own. Still, her hands gripped his shirt to give her something, anything, to hold onto.

'Lise.' His voice was a soft murmur. She didn't deserve this solace. The pain was something she should feel, but she couldn't move away, couldn't let him go. If she did, she might drown in it all. Sink beneath the waves of grief and never surface again. Rafe held her till her choked breaths eased and the threat of tears receded. She rested her head against his chest. Lulled by the steady thump of his heartbeat as he stroked her hair, saying nothing, merely holding her together. It was too easy to stand there in the safety of his arms, letting the warmth of him seep into her frozen places. To soak him in.

To hope for things that weren't for her.

She pushed away from his chest and his hold eased. His expression one of concern before she moved away and scrubbed at her eyes, rubbing at the few tears that had managed to escape.

'I'm fine. Really.' She turned to the view from the glass doors leading to the balcony. At a winding road, the spire of a little church, nestled in the rolling green foothills of the Alps. Looking at anything to avoid looking at him.

She felt Rafe's warmth behind her. His hands, rested on her shoulders. A gentle rub of his thumbs on her neck. Goosebumps shivered across her back and down her arms at his comforting touch. 'It's okay not to be. You've been through an ordeal. Take some time to grieve, whilst there's no one here to watch you.'

Yet unbeknownst to him, her losses were self-inflicted. Own goals. She shrugged him away. She had no right to his sympathy or the temptation of his touch, which made her want to fall into him and never get up again.

'I don't have the luxury of time.'

'You've a country to run. And you're exhausting yourself. There's no thanks in that.'

Rafe walked in front of her, cupped her face in his hands. 'Asking for help doesn't make you weak. It takes strength to know when you can't do it on your own.'

She wanted help. She wanted someone to rely on, something she'd never really had before. To allow her to feel more like herself. Not the broken woman. Not the Queen. Just Lise.

I'll give you anything you want...

He was asking for that person to be him and part of her, the dark secret heart of her, wished it could be. And those were dangerous, tempting thoughts to have.

Because Rafe was the last person she should ever trust.

CHAPTER SIX

LISE HUGGED HER knees as she sat in the verdant grass staring at the picturesque view over a valley. A little church, a quaint village, all surrounded by majestic Alpine peaks. She'd followed a short and well-worn trail, bringing her to this place with its outlook over the mountains. She'd attempted to call Sara, to check on her friend to see if she was okay, to try and talk too about her own conflicted emotions, but there had been no answer. The phone oddly going to a message bank that claimed to be full.

Lise flopped back and spread her arms wide, staring into the deepening blue sky above her. She should have worn something more suitable than light clothing and a flowing skirt for the walk, as the sun had begun dipping low, the air taking on a crisp early autumn chill. But the thought that she could simply wander away with no plan or agenda had been too tempting. As Queen, she was coming to learn there was always some agenda, always a plan. She shut her eyes, concentrating not on what she had to do but in this single, blissful moment. On the gentle chimes of cow bells in the distance, the tickle of grass under her fingers. The brush of a late afternoon breeze on her cheeks. Simple, honest pleasures that she could allow herself to indulge in.

The sense of some presence, that she was not alone, caused her to open her eyes and turn.

Rafe. Cutting a swathe through the swaying grasses, as he strolled in her direction. Lise's heart fluttered like the butterflies that had earlier been sampling the remaining wildflowers dotted around her.

'Hello, Sleeping Beauty. Did I wake you?' He smiled, and any remaining chill left the afternoon and she bathed in the warmth of him.

'I wasn't asleep, and no prince kissed me, so...'

What was she saying? His dark eyes gleamed in the golden light of a dropping sun and the corner of his mouth quirked into a wry grin.

'That could have been arranged, although you'd have to have settled for a king, rather than Prince Charming.'

'I'm not sure that's how the fairy tale goes.'

Lise couldn't help herself. She glanced at his mouth, the curve of his lower lip that seemed so soft and full, and wondered again what it would be like to kiss him, just once. For real, not only in her overheated fantasies.

'You're Queen, you could write your own.'

She shook her head. 'Life doesn't work like that.'

'In the end, life is what you make of it.' Rafe gestured to the ground next to her. 'May I join you?'

She nodded, and he sprawled beside her, plucking at the grass and flowers as he stared out over the landscape. Its magnificence paling in his distracting presence.

'You've found one of my favourite places here,' he said, pointing to the valley. 'The church is where generations of my family were married... and buried. I started my schooling in the village.'

'And now you rule all you survey.'

The corner of his mouth curled to a wry grin. 'This is my true home. I always believed I ruled here. The invincibility of youth.'

She stared out over the landscape. Not looking at him because his presence was a palpable thing that slipped under her skin, filling her with the pulse of desire. She craved to lean into Rafe's warmth and strength, absorb some into herself.

'It's somehow easier to think, up here,' she said. She breathed deeply for what felt like the first time in weeks. It was as if here, away from the capital, her knotted thoughts unspooled.

'And what are you thinking about?'

She might not be able to sink into his arms but surely she could share some of her fears? For all his faults and scheming, he had never failed to make her feel...*worthy*. One of the few people who ever did, and in a way she had truly believed.

Lise sat up, plucked a long blade of grass from before her and wound it round her finger.

'How can I rule a country when I was never shown the way? My purposes were only decorative. This role requires more than simply smiling and waving or cutting ribbons.' She cast the now crushed strand of grass away and hugged her knees to her chest. Of course, she wasn't simply planning to rule the country, but to move it towards a future without her or a royal family. Never again would someone be forced to take on a role they didn't aspire to simply because of a quirk of birth. To be forced to marry…

'Don't say that.' Rafe's voice was strong and sure. 'You may not have been trained as Queen, but *you've* trained. To push through pain and fear to win. Don't forget your skiing. You were slated to make the European championships. It shows a strength and commitment to succeed that others didn't display. You have a determination inside yourself. No one can take it away from you.'

'You make it sound so easy.'

'Was competition easy?'

She shook her head. It was gruelling and exhilarating and terrifying, but never easy.

'There's your answer.'

She turned to him and looked at his hands, his strong, capable fingers weaving the final touches to a wreath of grasses and wildflowers.

'What's that?'

'I used to have to make garlands for the cows in our autumn village festival, celebrating their descent from the mountains for winter.'

'You're making a cow crown?'

He chuckled and the warm, throaty sound rippled right through her.

'If I'm King of these mountains, *ruling all I survey*, then I need a queen.' Rafe held the wreath up to her cradled in his palms, then reached out and placed it gently on her head. 'And now, I have her.'

Something inside, a hard veneer that she'd shellacked over her heart, softened and cracked a little. The well of emotion, dangerously like hope, threatening to spill over inside her. 'It's so much lighter than the real thing.'

Rafe cocked his head, his gaze intent and assessing. 'You wear both crowns well, Lise. Never forget.'

Over his shoulder, a star winked on in the sky. She hadn't realised how quickly the sun was sinking below the horizon. This moment full of magic, she didn't want it to end. Just the two of them sitting here. Rafe and Lise. King and Queen of the mountains. In the fading light the breeze picked up and cut through her. She shivered.

'Come.' He stood up and held his hand out to her. She slipped her cool hand into his, engulfed by the heat of his palm as he helped her to her feet. How easy this was, to go to him. Hold hands and walk together towards the house as a real couple might. 'It's getting late and, even though the path is well worn, being out in the mountains at night can be treacherous. I also have dinner to make.'

Rafe released her hand as they entered the house. She immediately missed its warmth, the sense of comfort he provided. He kicked off his shoes at the door then moved to the rustic kitchen, with its copper pots and knots of herbs and garlic hanging from the ceiling. Rafe eased a cork from a bottle of wine. Poured a glass and slid it across the counter to her. Poured one for himself and raised it as if in a toast.

'Here's to a simple life. Good food, good wine, good company.'

She turned and toasted too then took a sip of the crisp, fragrant white. 'Well, we have one here. The wine's superb.'

He bowed. 'My latest acquisition.'

'But it's made by the oldest winery in the country.' They were world renowned and had won international awards. The business had been run by the family for close to a century. 'Why would they sell?'

Rafe crossed his arms, his biceps bulging in a distracting way as he did.

'They were crippled by red tape, lack of government assistance and cheap imports. There's been no care taken for the businesses that made our country great. They're being lost to overseas interests. I've been fighting to stop that happening. Maybe we can change the decline together? Reinvigorate the economy.'

'What's wrong with the economy?' Her father had never spoken to her of it, presumably because it had been unnecessary. In her brief weeks as Queen, no one had mentioned the economy at all.

'People have been lulled by complacency. It's time you shook them awake.' Rafe tilted his head, and his eyes narrowed a fraction. He remained a mystery in so many ways. Right now she couldn't read him at all. 'But enough. This weekend's about getting away from all that. We have the good wine. The good company. What we need is the good food.'

He took a wooden board from a hook, set it in front of her with a knife and a bowl of mushrooms in what seemed to be a deft change of subject. 'I've brushed off the detritus. Chop these into slices and we'll eat soon.'

It was as if he'd deflected her question. Part of her felt dismissed, although another part didn't want to contemplate right now what it took to run the country. She wanted to simply take a breath. *Be*. Time enough for the business of ruling Lauritania a bit later. It was only a few days.

'What are we having?' she asked, slicing through the mushrooms.

'Not the cordon bleu of the palace. Something more rustic.'

'I'll let you in on a secret,' she said, taking another sip of her wine before chopping more mushrooms, 'That's the type of food I wish I could cook.'

He raised his eyebrows. 'What did finishing school teach you if not how to feed yourself? It seems like the sort of basic skill a person should learn.'

'Apart from flower arranging and correct placement of cutlery, I'm an expert on theatrical dishes like bombe Alaska or crêpes Suzette. Of course, if I want to eat anything other than extravagant desserts for the rest of my life, I'm doomed.'

'Never with me. I'll save you from starvation,' he said with the flourish of a spatula and a grin that lit a glow inside her. Reminding her of the breathtaking man she'd craved with something of an obsession. He was handsome all the time, devastating when he smiled.

She put her hand to her chest. 'My hero. In a palace with a kitchen full of chefs, you're the one who'll poach me an egg if I want it.'

He tossed some butter into a pan and it sizzled as he seared some sort of meat. Once that was done, she handed him a bowl of finely sliced mushrooms and he added them into the pan with an onion he'd already chopped.

'I'm afraid my heroic status is a myth. I've never mastered egg poaching. Veal with mushroom cream sauce is more my style.' Her mouth watered at the mere thought of that meal, and an appetite she'd forgotten resurfaced with a low grumble in her stomach. Lise took another sip of wine as Rafe drizzled some of his own into the pan and tossed the mushrooms with a practised skill.

'Impressive,' she said. And he was, in all ways. Commanding the kitchen, no doubt as he commanded the boardroom. And she realised she'd never really seen him in anything much other than business clothes. Not like this, in jeans with a casual shirt, cooking in a kitchen and looking… human. It was something of a shock to her system. She placed her now empty glass on the countertop and Rafe poured some more wine into it.

'I could teach you.'

'I think I'll just watch.' And she needed to watch him. This relaxed man, at ease with himself and in charge of everything around him, was a risk. She'd made commitments to herself. Nowhere in those was allowing him to slide under her skin.

He plated up the meal with a tidy twist of pasta and sprinkle of fresh herbs. Took both plates to an antique table, which carried the scars of many a meal prepared and eaten on its surface. In the centre sat a small cut-glass vase overflowing with wildflowers. A candle, which he lit. It looked cosy, romantic.

Dangerous.

'This is…' *Lovely.* 'Unnecessary.'

'We're having a simple meal, Lise, that's all.'

But there was nothing simple about this. The soft light. The warm room cocooning them. It was as if they were the only two people in the world. A world where they were not Queen and King of a whole country, but simply Lise and Rafe, rulers of the mountains. A tempting fantasy she had to ignore. They *were* Queen and King, and that reality would never change. She reached up and removed the beautiful grass and flower garland from her head as she sat, placing it on the table next to her.

Rafe raised an eyebrow, fixed her with a heated gaze. 'Shame, you looked beautiful.'

She tried to ignore the delicious thrill that ran through her at his words.

'One does not wear one's crown to a private dinner,' she said, in her most queenly tone, before taking a mouthful of food to avoid the moment. The rich flavour of mushrooms burst against her tongue. Lise caught a moan in the back of her throat. Rafe's gaze turned incendiary.

'You approve?'

She nodded, washed the mouthful down with another sip of wine. When had she last enjoyed anything she'd eaten? When had any food tasted more than dust on her tongue?

'We make a good team,' he said.

'How so?'

'Your mushroom-cutting skills are superlative.'

She laughed. 'Who'd have thought that was a skill I needed to learn?' She leaned back in her chair, relishing the food on her plate, the sharp edges of life softened by the wine in her ever-topped-up glass. After she finished, he cleared away and rinsed their plates. Wouldn't let her help. Motioned to the couch that sat squashed and low in front of the flickering fire. He took another board with a slab of cheese and placed it on the hearth.

The light danced in the room, painting his skin gold. Rafe's eyes dark and sultry. She sank into her end of the couch. He sprawled next to her, feet bare and propped on the coffee table in front of them. She'd never seen a man's naked feet. An odd sort of realisation that she'd always been faced with men in suits and polished shoes. Something about that made the evening seem even more intimate.

'I can see why you come here,' she said, trying not to think about any part of Rafe naked.

There was no sound bar the pop and crackle of the flames in the grate. She tipped her head back and stared up at the ceiling, the rough-hewn beams and white plaster in between, that had seen his family raised here. The man himself, this place that made him. Something about that was real, and grounding. A connection to the past she seemed divorced from, even though her family had ruled the country for centuries.

'As I've said, the mountains are my home. No matter where in the world I am, it's here I think of.'

He stared into the flames, took a sip of his wine. She watched the masculine bob of his Adam's apple as he swallowed.

She nodded. 'It's why I skied. I could get away from myself. The mountains don't allow any ego.'

'They don't accept mistakes. And they'll be here long after we're gone.'

'It's the one time I could feel alone. Challenge myself.'

He turned to her, his eyelids low and shuttered. 'What have you replaced the challenge with?'

'Isn't Queen enough?'

'That's a duty for others. What about for yourself?'

She remembered that day, the day everything had been set in train. When she'd only thought about herself and nothing else. She hadn't realised, in those moments, what she'd lose.

'There isn't anything more.'

He reached over and placed a hand over hers. She wanted to pull away, but somehow couldn't move, relishing the solidity of his touch.

'To be a good ruler you must allow something for yourself, or you'll cease to care. Not today, not tomorrow, but some day. Then the decisions you make won't come from the good of your heart, and they'll be the wrong ones. For your country. For your people. For you.'

What was he alluding to here? Her vow that the monarchy died with her? Lise shook her head. She didn't know what to take for herself. How was there anything left when everything had been stolen from her family? Where did she even start? With wine, perhaps. Maybe with another sip, a simple choice. She could do that, in the glass that Rafe seemed to ever fill.

The man in question left the couch and moved over to the cheese board close to the fire and cut off a now molten piece. He slathered it onto some crusty bread and held it out to her.

She shook her head. 'I couldn't.'

Though the glistening, molten cheese and bread looked tempting...

'One bite. My family made it,' he said. 'I'll eat the rest if you don't want to.'

Lise took a bite, teeth crunching in the crisp white bread. The cheese oozing everywhere. She gave a low moan of pleasure at the salty tang, then handed the bread back to him. His eyes darkened as he ate the rest himself.

'It's my idea of dessert,' he said. 'You can keep crêpe Suzette and bombe Alaska to yourself.'

'You don't like sweet things?'

He sat on the coffee table in front of her. Their knees brushing, sending a thrill through her. The fire flickering, glowing like a halo behind him.

Except the man was no angel.

'I indulge in some.' Rafe's voice was soft and smooth, like silk against her skin. He didn't take his eyes from her, as if he were trying to stare deep inside. Into all her secrets. He didn't need to do that; he knew enough of them to be a danger to her. Her heart beat a thready rhythm, and the breath caught in her throat. She reached round him to take her glass of wine, breaking eye contact.

'I'll keep that in mind. Any time I want to cook, it won't be dessert.'

'I didn't say I didn't like dessert, Lise. I'm merely selective in my choice of indulgence.'

He moved away from her now, and she let out a long, slow breath. Trying to forget the feel of him holding her as she fell apart this afternoon. Weaving her a floral crown, holding her hand as they walked to the house. The closeness that didn't feel feigned. In her deepest heart that was what she wanted for herself.

Rafe cut off more cheese, held it up. She shook her head. The room was warm, the couch soft and deep. Everything here cushioned her from the reality outside. The sharp edges of life a bit rounder, burnished smooth. And Rafe. The black curls gleaming in the low light. His hair all unruly as if it never behaved. A lot like the man himself. A passionate man, from all the envious whispers she'd overheard when he'd begun to pay her exclusive attention. A warm flush bled over her. She closed her eyes, to block him out, but it didn't work. Felt the couch dip, the heat of him closer. He slid an arm round her shoulders. She opened her eyes and glanced at the hand casually sitting along the back of the couch near her. The sprinkling of hair. The square-cut nails with perfect half-moons. When had a hand held so much fascination? He eased her closer, till she leaned on the side of him, tucked under his arm.

'Relax, Lise. Close your eyes if you want.'

'I don't want to sleep.'

He didn't feel safe. But neither had skiing on the black runs and that had made her stomach swoop and her heart pound. Never knowing what would come round the next bend. This was a little like that, the thrill of anticipation skittering through her belly. It was what she'd been missing, and she craved it like a drug. When had she stopped taking risks? Perhaps she could accept this, for a little while. She'd so wanted him to hold her, kiss her, before it all. The day of her wedding her only chance. She drank the rest of her wine. Rafe took the glass from her hands and set it on a table, before settling her into him again.

He'd wanted her. He'd made it clear. Why *not* kiss her on their wedding day when he'd had the perfect excuse? When she couldn't have said no, not in front of their guests and the millions watching on television. His answer to that question seemed imperative.

'You could have kissed me in the cathedral, yet you didn't. Why?'

She felt his lips at her hair. The warm breath of his murmur.

'You said it wasn't that kind of marriage.'

He was feigning obedience now? She snorted. 'I don't believe that. Your recalcitrance is renowned.'

He chuckled, and the sound ran like a dark river of pleasure running right through her. 'I wasn't kissing you in front of all those people.'

She turned to look at him. His face, dark and serious. His eyes intent.

'Why?'

'I refused to share what you say would have been our only kiss with the world.' He cupped her jaw with his hand, so warm, so close. His voice a whisper on her skin. 'Because I couldn't kiss you then the way I wanted to.'

His thumb caressed her cheek, the gentle back and forth sprinkling goosebumps over her body. All of her trembling, tight and wanting. How had he wanted to kiss her? Why couldn't it be done before the cameras? She had to know. Now craving their first and only kiss, more necessary than her next heartbeat.

'You could do it now, like you wanted to.'

Rafe's nostrils flared. His thumb stilled for a moment and resumed its slow slide across her skin. 'You claimed it wasn't what you wanted.'

'It's not.' He raised an eyebrow. 'But, I mean, I shouldn't deny you our first and only kiss. It wouldn't be fair.'

'You're asking me to kiss you?'

'Yes. It's no big deal. It's only a kiss.'

The hint of a smile tugged at his lips before his face became serious, intent. Staring deep into her eyes. His, an inky black like Lake Morenberg on a moonlit night. Deep, unreachable, unfathomable. A look that delved into the soul of her. She couldn't have that. What he'd see. She closed her eyes so that she couldn't be impaled by that all-knowing gaze.

'No. If we're going to kiss, look at me.'

It was the demand of a king, and it shook

through her like a tremor, cracking at the foundations of everything Lise believed she wanted. She obeyed, their heated gazes clashing. The firelight sparking in his eyes making him seem otherworldly. Unholy. The moment stretched, as if the evening held its breath.

'One kiss,' he murmured, easing closer. Closing the gap between them. His lips soft, with a satisfied curve that screamed to her he believed he'd won. Yet she didn't care. This was better than standing at the top of a run, waiting for the signal to push off and fly as fast as she could to the finish line. It all overwhelmed her. The crisp, wild smell of him. The tight clench of his jaw and flickering pulse in his throat that hinted he wasn't unaffected by this as he eased closer. Giving her time to say no, as his mouth was a breath away from hers. She closed the distance till his lips brushed hers, which she met with a sharp inhale. The shock of that first touch. Then he pressed further. Gentle, coaxing her to life with a bright burst of heat deep inside.

She went with him, her stomach swooping as if she'd launched down the steepest of slopes. The flame roaring through her as if he'd ignited a fuse. It was okay. This was just a kiss, one kiss as he teased at her. She wanted more, not this furtive play. She sank her hands into his hair. He deepened the movement. Traced his tongue over the seam of her lips in a flicker. She opened her mouth and he claimed it. The tip of his tongue tempting hers in an intimate invasion. She chased it, gripped by a need that overtook her as Rafe plundered. This wasn't just one kiss. This *consumed* her.

He eased her back onto the couch and she offered no resistance, wanting and wanting. Rafe settled between her thighs. The hardness of his body hot between her legs. The heart of her turned molten. Something inside twisting higher and tighter. She rocked against his body. Craving this. Craving him. The voice in the back of her head whispered *no*. She didn't deserve the pleasure. But it was drowned by a deepening of the kiss, the exploration of his tongue, as if he sensed her withdrawal from him. How could she ignore it? This wicked thrill as she raced downhill into the chaos of it all. Pressed underneath Rafe, being kissed by him. Could she come like this alone? She might. She could. To the left, slightly. If she could just… Lise shifted restlessly. She needed him close. Closer. *Inside her.*

Rafe rocked into her, grinding his body on hers. His mouth claiming. This was no kiss. It destroyed her and she didn't care. She wanted to destroy Rafe in the process too, as the course he'd set ran out of control. An avalanche of sensations burying her.

She tore her mouth from his. 'Rafe. I want—'

'Tell me.' His voice was all command and the thrill of its mastery shuddered through her.

'I need you.' Who was the woman who said those words? The breathless, desperate woman whose voice whispered months of longing, heartbreak and desire. His mouth descended on hers again. She felt the taut curve of a smile against her lips. It could have been one of triumph, or something else. She didn't care. In this moment she lived for the dissonance of his hard body against hers.

He eased a hand under her top, the warmth of it still a shock even on her overheated flesh. The trace of his fingers across her skin. He moved up, slipping his hand behind to release her from the constraints of her bra, all the while kissing as if his life would end if he didn't plunder her.

She wrapped her legs around him, unable to control the rock as she moved her body with his. Chasing the liquid heat between her thighs. The feel of him burning through her. Starting low and igniting the fire. His hand slid further, moving the cup of her bra aside, teasing her nipple with a gentle roll between his fingers. She started as if shocked, but he'd trapped her mouth and the low groan from it, as if taking it all for himself. She craved nothing between them, squirming beneath his body, needing more, needing to be close. Her hands under his shirt now, the hard muscles under her palms, the hiss as she curled her nails into the flexing muscles of his back. Hands bunching the shirt at his waist reflexively. He pulled his lips away from her and she whimpered, not wanting any part of him to leave her body.

'Take it off me.'

The gravel voice scored across her, as rough and raw as she felt. She clutched the bottom of his shirt and pulled it up over his shoulders. He lifted for a moment and sat back, discarding the clothing onto the floor. His body golden in the firelight. Hard muscle, with that intoxicating sprinkle of hair across his chest. His eyes on her, all dark heat. Nostrils flaring and he was primal, like some wild untamed thing reserving his passion all for her.

'Now you.' Again, a command. He gave her no time to follow it. His hands gripping her top and easing it over her head. Taking her bra with it. She lay, exposed. He hissed, his gaze raking over her as her nipples ruched tight and needy in the night air.

Under his scrutiny, she shifted uncomfortably. The promises she'd made herself pricking at her consciousness now that the fog of Rafe had lifted a fraction. She shifted an arm, to cover herself, and he grasped the hand and pinned it above her head. A flood of heat roared through her at the dominant move. She couldn't breathe, every inhale a brief suck of air because he stole all the oxygen from the room.

'This is the dessert I prefer.' His eyes held hers. 'Look at you, laid out for me like a feast.'

His hand drifted low, easing up the hem of her skirt. She should stop him. Push him away because of the promises she'd made. To herself.

'Rafe.'

His name came out high-pitched. A breathy plea. He released her trapped hand, and his free fingers trailed her stomach. Lower and lower till they teased the edge of her underwear. Her hips bucked into him. Wanting, craving his fingers to ease the burn that bit with the edge of pain.

'Shh... I know. I'll take care of you.'

No one ever had and she wanted it, wanted him to make everything better. He slid his fingers underneath the edge of her panties. Gentle, teasing lower and lower till they found the spot she craved. She arched, head thrown back. Gasping as he circled. Everything centred on that point between her legs. The craving that consumed her. The noises she made. Moving her hips in time with the inexorable swirl of his fingers as he drew on her slick, desperate flesh.

And any thoughts of promises were blinded in the bright light of pleasure that gripped her body and began an inexorable spiral tighter. He lay on his side now, beside her, stroking her. Murmuring she didn't know what because language was meaningless in the face of this. The deep dark tone of his voice inflaming her as much as his fingers did. Then he drifted his hand further, to the entrance of her body. Slid inside. One finger. Withdrew. Two. Touching some place deep inside. Making her trembling and frantic. Every nerve screaming for the release only he could give her.

'Please, please, Rafe.'

'You deserve kisses, everywhere.'

'I need more.'

Through fluttering lashes, the haze of arousal, his triumphant smile cut through. She didn't care. Everything centred on his touch. The heat of it scorched her. Burning between her thighs. She clutched them together because the ache threatened to overwhelm her. Rafe bore down. Eyes all fire and dark desire. He took one nipple in his mouth. His tongue swirling. When she thought he couldn't ignite more heat inside her, she realised how wrong she was. Then her left nipple. His tongue making a slow trail down the centre of her stomach. Soft kisses and licks. Lower and lower still. Her hips squirmed, he gripped them with strong, warm hands.

'Open for me.'

Her legs relaxed. He kissed her inner thigh, up and up. Till he was there. *There*. His breath warm at the apex of her thighs. The touch of his lips, light and gentle. Then his tongue. She arched back. Light exploding behind her eyes. The pleasure. He didn't stop the slow slide, the tcase driving her wild. Everything centred on him, between her legs. A finger now, easing inside. And nothing could hold back the brutal pleasure that built and built and roared over her as she held her breath, clenched her hands tight and rode wave after wave of trembling ecstasy.

He moved over her, his weight pressing her into the couch. His lips on hers, the salt sweet of her own arousal. The thrum of desire still coursing through her. Rafe had broken her apart. She'd been lulled by a belief that a kiss with this man could be so simple, when Rafe was anything but. A cold thread of recrimination wound through her veins. Dark, destructive. The desire that had overwhelmed her, flooding her with an intoxicating warmth, disappeared as if she'd been doused with frigid water.

Before she could push Rafe away he stopped, broke the kiss, gazed down at her with dark eyes burning hot like the fallen embers in the fireplace.

'I want you. To be inside you,' he murmured, and his voice slid over her like midnight velvet. 'What do you want?'

It would be so easy to whisper the word, *you*. He had the power to make her forget everything, but she hadn't earned that right.

She never would.

'Off. Please.' Her hands splayed on the warmth of his naked chest, the crisp hair teasing under her fingertips, but she didn't push him away. He was the one to move. Lifting from her. Sitting back on the couch as he dropped his head and raked his hands through his hair.

'Lise.' Her name on his lips was like a groan. Impassioned. Pained. Stabbing through the very heart of her. All this interlude had proven was that she was weak. Once again, her self-interest had guided her.

What sort of Queen was she if she couldn't keep vows to the dead?

'I can't… I *can't.*'

She stood, naked in body and soul. Rafe would see right through her if he looked hard enough. He always had.

Lise didn't stop. Didn't collect her clothes. She turned and fled up the stairs.

Rafe stood in the country kitchen, gulping down a strong, black coffee, Lise's grass and flower crown withering on the benchtop. How magical she'd looked crowned in flowers, like the hopeful Princess he'd known her to be before life overtook them both. It had seemed like a new beginning, till everything fell apart again.

He glanced at the staircase, at the clock ticking away the hours on the wall. The cold of a brisk, mountain morning nipped at his exposed skin. He'd not slept last night. Listening for any sound from Lise. Alert to every creak and crack of the ancient floors, which in his fevered fantasies meant she was coming to him to finish what they'd started, all the while drowning in the frustration of lust and desire unfulfilled. He'd had plenty of that over the years since he'd first set his sights on Lise but now... Cataloguing those moments on the couch, the taste of her pleasure, the sound. The scent of her arousal that he couldn't wash away.

That he never wanted to.

He could have gone to her, but the memory of that tortured look on her face as she'd said, *'I can't,'* stopped him. He'd rushed her. Rather than taking one step forwards he'd tried to run a marathon. He was a man renowned for his patience and strategy and he'd failed in all ways last night, overcome by the craving to make her *his* in every way. All he was left with this morning was the burn of regret, when he'd spent his life after Carl's death ensuring that he regretted nothing.

The clock chimed nine. He didn't believe Lise was still asleep, and they couldn't avoid what had happened the night before. He needed a reset so he could understand why she refused anything that might give her pleasure. So they could begin again.

He poured a cup of coffee for her, as she preferred. Plenty of milk. Sugar. Then walked up the stairs and knocked at the door of her room. Silence. He knocked again, then opened the door a sliver and peered inside.

The fire had died overnight, the room gripped in a morning chill. But that wasn't what caused the shiver to run over him. It was Lise, huddled in the corner velvet couch, staring into the dead fireplace. Her shoulders bare.

'You should be in bed. It's freezing out there. I've brought you a coffee.'

He came into the room. Lise didn't move as he rounded the couch. She wore a pink slip, her nipples tight against the silken fabric. Her skin pale and white as midwinter snowfall. How long had she been sitting here, staring into the fireplace? He glanced at the bed, the covers in disarray, twisted and knotted like his. As if she'd not slept at all.

She wrapped her arms tight around her knees, as if she was trying to protect herself against something. Rafe walked towards her. Lise's focus remained intent on the dark, dead fireplace as if the secrets of the universe could be divined there. Her nose a little pink, her eyes swollen. Whatever gripped her, it wasn't a conversation he could have like this. He picked up a folded rug from the arm of the chair.

'You need something to keep you warm.'

'No.' He barely heard the word; it came out on a breath.

As he sat on the couch, she pressed herself further into the corner, away from him. He placed her coffee on a side table, gut twisting in concern. 'What's wrong, Lise?'

Her recent life had been full of too many tears. He wished there were a way to obliterate the pain that burrowed deep inside her.

'I told you. How this marriage had to be. I told you.'

It still didn't make sense. How could she maintain the desire to live life untouched after last night? For those brief moments spasming in ecstasy under his ministrations, she'd been *his*. Completely, enthusiastically. Yet now, she was further away from him than ever.

'Things change. There's no crime in passion.'

'What if we had sex? What if I fell *pregnant*?' She spat out the word as if the thought of having his child was an insult. 'It's what you want, isn't it? The "heir and a spare or two"?'

He'd inured himself to most rejections over the years, but that statement still twisted like a knife under the ribs. The poisonous words crept into his consciousness. The sneer, the rejection, the laughter. *'Rafe, what we've had is a little bit of fun—but marry you...?'* None of the women of

Lauritania's aristocracy had wanted any permanence, not with him. The commoner. No matter those families were now close to bankrupt. That he owned them, owned everything they had. They still pretended they were better than him. Why should he think she would be any different? She was more than a mere noblewoman. She was the *Queen*. He gritted his teeth, tamped down the twist in his gut. Those memories, those thoughts, had no place here. He'd moved past them. He had.

'Would it be so bad if you had a baby?' Rafe loathed his question, what it revealed of him. It was what he craved, cementing his family on the seat of his country's power for generations to come.

A shudder ran through her. 'I don't want a daughter brought into the world I inhabit. I'll never do to a girl what was forced upon me as Queen.'

He ignored the slice of rejection. She hadn't been allowed to find her own way, that was all. And he of all people understood Lise's need to make a place for herself, to carve her own path. Time to remind her she could.

'You can be the catalyst for change, so you're the last Queen this happens to. We can do it, together. Bring Lauritania into the twenty-first century.'

'You have so much faith in me.'

'Because I know you. You're in your rightful place. Ruling the country is exactly where you should be. You're wasted anywhere else.'

He edged closer to her, still with the blanket in hand. Her knuckles blanched white as her hands gripped more tightly round her bent legs.

'I'm an impostor,' Lise said. 'I failed my family.'

She shivered, goosebumps peppering her skin. Lips, pale and dusky. Why sit there in the cold? They could have carried on last night. Spent it together, pleasuring each other till dawn broke and they slept from exhaustion, truly spent. They could have been warm in bed right now and yet she'd refused it. Refused comfort. It was as if she were punishing herself.

And the realisation came like dawn breaking over the mountain peaks. Lise punished herself for living.

He was a fool for not realising it before, because he understood all too well. He had a choice. To leave her paralysed with grief or to share a little of himself in the hope it would help. Give her something that granted a power few had over him. Rafe stood to stoke the fire. Collect his thoughts on a story etched into his soul.

Only his family and Lance knew how deep the pain scored. People at school had taunted his memories, but to them Carl was soon forgotten.

His brother's only use being the vehicle by which to hurt Rafe in his grief.

'I understand why you feel like this,' he said.

Rafe jabbed at a few bright coals still hiding in the hearth, coaxing them to life. Wishing he could do the same with Lise as easily. He added a few more logs till the fire crackled bright and warm then sat down again.

'You've no idea,' she whispered.

'Every day for the past fifteen years I've wished I had no idea what you're feeling.' He could never escape the things he rarely talked about because the memories were too painful. Rafe lifted the blanket he held and passed it to Lise. 'I want to tell you a story about two brothers. But before I do, you need to be warm.'

His offering didn't seem enough. Yet she wrapped the blanket, crocheted by his grand-mother, round herself. The wool would prickle against her soft skin, but at least she wouldn't sit there shivering, uncovered.

'I'm not an only child. I had a brother once. He was a year younger than me.' Rafe loathed talking about him in the past tense, because he carried Carl with him every day. 'He died in an accident when I was sixteen.'

The pain of the memory impaled him. He draped his arm over the back of the couch. His hand lay tantalisingly close to the gentle curve of

Lise's neck. She chewed on her bottom lip, but there was a flicker of recognition on her face and something else. A spark of something brighter, like hope that there might be burdens they could share.

'Carl?'

Rafe nodded, swallowing down the emotion at hearing Lise say his name.

'When I went to the Kings' Academy, all the sons of the aristocracy loathed me. Our family wasn't poor, but our money came from physical work, not exalted inheritance. I sullied their hallowed halls.' Teachers had told his parents he was destined for bigger and better things than a farming life but all he'd learned at that school was hatred and prejudice. 'Bullying was rife and brutal, but I taught myself how to fight back. Then my life became less about the farm and more about studying, to be better.'

To beat them all. And he had. Topping every class. Then he'd met Lance and they'd become an unassailable force. The boys at that school had only hated him more. He hadn't cared. In his last year he'd been dux of the school, had received an outstanding achievement award from the King himself.

'Carl did not fare as well. He was a gentle, quiet boy. I think he liked the herd better than people.' Even Rafe had taunted him about that, something he regretted to this day. 'The bullying was relent-less. Carl didn't understand why the boys would never be friends with him. He failed his classes, begged to be sent home. My parents removed him from the school. If only he'd remained...'

Rafe hesitated, the pain blunting only a frac-tion, even after all these years. He glanced a Lise, a slight frown marring her brow. She reached over and squeezed his hand, that small comfort giving him the impetus to continue.

'It was during term time. We'd lost two of our best milkers. Carl was going to hike the mountain pastures to try and find them. Night fell, and he didn't come home...'

'And nights on the mountain can be treacher-ous, even if you're on a well-worn path,' Lise said. He nodded.

'I received a call at the school that night. Was sent home to join in the search.' Rafe dropped his head. The memory of a crumpled body at the bottom of a steep slope would haunt him for ever.

'We found him the next morning. Carl was taken to hospital and died a few days later with-out regaining consciousness. The damned cows made their way home themselves.

'I wanted to leave school. My parents wouldn't listen. If I'd protected him from the bullying. If he'd remained a student rather than returning home. If...' Rafe dropped his head. Closed his eyes. Trying to ignore the burn that stung the back of his nose.

'It was an accident. It wasn't your fault.' Lise's voice rang out firm and clear.

He knew that now. Back then, he'd believed that had he protected his brother, Carl would have lived. The truth lay somewhere in between. Carl had not been cut out for the Kings' Academy, bullying or no, and the way he'd loved wandering the mountain pastures there had always been a chance he'd come to grief. Though in those years afterwards Rafe had blamed himself with a savagery that had almost torn him apart. Till his parents had hauled him aside, told him they loved him and that, with his grief and rage, they feared losing not one son, but two. From that point on he'd decided he couldn't change the past, but he could try to change the future.

He cleared his throat of the emotion choked there. 'Like your family. A mountain pass. A rock fall. So why blame yourself? Blame Security for allowing them to travel together.'

Lise trembled, the look on her face once again so bereft he thought she'd fall apart. No more of this distance. He couldn't stand it, not when they both needed each other. He drew her into his arms. She came to him without resistance. He held her close as she curled into his chest, her skin cold against him. He wrapped the blanket tighter round her. Soothed his hands over her quaking body.

'Ferdinand never got his chance,' she said. 'He was going to be married. Sara...'

She clung to him. What could he tell her—that her brother was a serial philanderer and that her best friend had had a lucky escape to be rid of him? No. He wouldn't hurt her any more than she already was, he wasn't that cruel. Better that she believe the illusion for now, that her brother and his fiancée were a grand love, fated to be rather than cursed from the beginning.

'Sara's a young woman with her whole life ahead of her to live and love.' *Like you*, but he didn't voice those words. She wouldn't appreciate the truth of them, that, whilst the pain wouldn't disappear, she *would* carry on. She had to come to the realisation herself. 'All we have are these brief moments. Sometimes to remember. Other times to forget.'

He stroked his fingers along her jaw, rewarded by her parted lips and soft exhale as he did.

'I can help you with the forgetting,' he murmured, threading his fingers into her hair before he could think that it might not have been wise, considering her earlier reaction. Drawn to Lise in ways that defied logical thought. It was as if, after last night, he couldn't *not* touch her. Craving to ease her pain.

She pulled her head back and looked up at him with her cool blue eyes. What did she see when she did that? It was as if they opened the door to his soul, that celestial colour. Then she shook her head. Disentangled herself from him. Yet again he had to let her go when all of him shouted *no!* That what she needed was closeness, not distance.

'There's never any forgetting, Rafe. Not for me. Your presence will always make me remember.' She stood, holding her back straight, her head high. The crocheted blanket slid from her shoulders. Even in a scant slip of nightwear, looking pale and fragile, she still had the bearing of a queen. Lise turned and headed to the door of the room. As she reached it, she hesitated. 'You should have realised. That's precisely why I married you.'

As she left the room, he knew in those moments he'd been summarily dismissed. There were undercurrents here he couldn't understand and needed to get to the bottom of. But an unshakeable knowledge spread over him with a bone-cracking chill.

She'd married him as part of her penalty for living.

CHAPTER SEVEN

THREE DAYS AWAY, and they'd returned to the palace with its timetables and strictures. Lise was torn. For a brief time she had found a measure of peace, away from the capital. Those days were like an oasis of calm in the middle of a wasteland of grief. She hadn't wanted to leave the tranquillity of Rafe's home in the mountains, where she might once have pretended they were simply a man and a woman united by shared grief, and not who they truly were. A man who wanted power from a beneficial marriage and a woman forced to marry by her constitution. No matter what Rafe had shared with her, that was their truth. They were who they were, and life wasn't all glitter-covered fantasises but full of harsh realities. Living with the dark, twisting ache that she didn't deserve any meagre shred of happiness.

Yet her pain had dissipated to a background hum in the fog of passion in Rafe's arms. All she could think about was what he'd done to her. The exquisite sensation of his mouth on the heart of her, the way she'd broken apart under his wicked tongue. Her craving for more, for *everything*. The heat rose in her chest, and she was sure the blush bloomed over her face.

'They call this informal?'

Her stomach swooped as Rafe walked into the dining room. He'd taken a call for business and hadn't followed her to breakfast, so she'd thought she'd have longer to eat without him. At least in the mountains she could walk the narrow cattle trails to escape. To create a little space, since being back in the palace allowed her none. Here, togetherness was everything. The illusion of Queen and King working together for the good of the country.

The man in question glowered as he looked at the expansive table, set in full silver service for two. Lise sat at one end. A place for him lay at the other where a patch of sunshine hit the table. In front of the setting lay perfectly pressed newspapers. If it weren't so real, it might have been comical.

'We're serving ourselves. Here, that's almost considered to be camping.' The laden buffet could have fed a family of ten, rather than the two of them. Though she hadn't eaten much of the magnificent meal set out on the sideboard. Since they'd returned to the palace her stomach had recommenced twisting itself into complicated and uncomfortable knots.

Rafe snorted. 'I'm not sitting so far away we need to phone each other to speak.' He strode to his end of the table, grabbed the cutlery and newspapers and placed them next to Lise. 'It's ridiculous.'

She nodded to the end of the table he'd vacated.

'That was my father's place. He liked to read the paper in the sunshine.' Lise sipped her coffee. 'My mother sat here because she said the sun ruined her skin.'

'I'm not your father.'

The memory of the King, sitting at the end of the table poring through the papers, sliced like a shard of glass. But her father wasn't here any more and, no, Rafe was most definitely *not* him. No man of her family would have worn jeans to the breakfast table. Even very fine jeans, that hung low on the hips and showed off the distracting vee of a man's torso. Nor would they ever have worn a business shirt with the sleeves rolled up. Rolled-up sleeves would have been sacrilege and meant showing muscular arms. If they'd even had muscles, which she wasn't convinced of, but Rafe most definitely did. The magnificent swell of his biceps when his shirt was removed, his powerful chest. The corded tendons straining as he'd dropped his head between her legs and...

'Lise?'

He was standing at the sideboard now, plate loaded with food. He probably needed to eat quite a bit, to keep his energy up for...all the things she refused to think about at this moment because she was becoming quite obsessed with ideas of Rafe permanently shirtless.

'I'm sorry. Yes?'

The corner of his mouth tilted in a lopsided grin as he strolled back to the table. Could he tell what she'd been thinking? No doubt. She'd bet the Crown jewels he knew *exactly* what had been distracting her. He placed his plate on the tabletop.

'I said, to me, an informal breakfast suggests something like breakfast in bed.'

Swoop. Her stomach dropped once more and her heart took off at a race. The feeling more intoxicating than slaloming cross-country through trees. And more dangerous.

She nibbled a bread roll and took another sip of coffee. 'I'm sure breakfast in bed has never been served in the palace. It's not done.'

Rafe hadn't sat down. He moved towards her, and she was forced to tilt her head up to meet his gaze. 'Use your magisterial powers to order breakfast in bed and make it so.'

Could he see the desire that curled slow and hot through her belly? Winding deep and low on a seductive journey that made her thighs clench together and her nipples bud and prickle in her bra.

'For both of us?' Her voice came out as a breathy whisper. It sounded like an invitation when she meant they could both dine alone in their respective rooms, didn't she?

'Perhaps you could join me? My bed is bigger. A perfect place to consume a sumptuous meal.' Her breath caught when he dropped his head to hers. His lips at her ear, his words caressing her throat as he murmured, 'More room to indulge in…eating what I prefer.'

She closed her eyes, memories cascading over her like a flood of warm water. Rafe, holding her hands above her head. Pinning her with his dark and heated gaze.

'Look at you, laid out for me like a feast.'

He could spread her out, here on the table. There was no one to see them…

A subtle cough behind her jolted Lise from the addictive fantasy. Rafe whispered into her ear, 'Breakfast in bed tomorrow.'

It wasn't a request and the decadent promise in his voice threatened to liquefy her bones, till she slid off the chair and melted in a puddle on the floor. She was sure none of that was at all regal of her. Queens didn't melt or swoon.

Rafe didn't seem likewise affected. He turned to the butler who stood behind them and raised his eyebrow in a supercilious way even her father would have been challenged to replicate.

'Yes?'

'Coffee, Your Majesty?'

'Thank you.' Rafe nodded and sat to eat as his coffee was poured. Rifling through the newspapers spread out in front of him. She hated the papers now, talking about her on the front page, every day...

'The narrative reads well.' Rafe took a long sip from his cup. Closed his eyes for a moment as if savouring the drink, then concentrated on the news again.

'What do you mean?'

He turned one towards her. A picture of them in Rafe's car returning to the palace. Both of them smiling at something. She couldn't remember the moment, but there it was, caught on camera for everyone to see, with words about a 'romantic escape' and 'new era'.

'Running a country's like running a billion-dollar company. Shareholders are most confident when the management's working together. Your people are most happy if they believe we are.'

Of course, with him, everything reverted to business. Even their relationship, such as it was. Fodder for the hungry masses. This thing between them, nothing more than an illusion of happiness. She was just another deal to him.

'I'm pleased we can give everyone the pretence.' She scrunched the napkin on her lap. Tossed it to the table. Swallowed down a different sort of ache, a sharp kind of hurt that sliced away inside. Paring away pieces of her. That was always her value, as part of the business of the Crown, not as a flesh and blood woman. Never that. She stood, wanting to escape the tightening inside her. 'I think I'll go for a run. Or a swim.'

Rafe stood as well. 'It's not a pretence for me. I hope one day you feel the same.'

'Yes, if I did it would help fit with the narrative you're so fond of.' She waved her hand over the papers on the table. Hating that this was what her life had become.

'There's a lot to being a monarch that's deliberate and calculated.' He caught her fingers, traced his thumb gently over the back of her hand. Beyond her control a thrill of goosebumps shimmied along her arm. 'It doesn't mean you don't deserve to feel something real.'

'I'll keep that in mind.' She slid her hand out from his, confused. He could be so passionate, all consuming. Then so businesslike and circumspect. It was hard to pin down who the real man was.

Another of the palace staff came into the room and Rafe slipped his arm round her waist. Dipped his head and gently kissed her cheek. Her skin tingled where his lips had touched but this was all for show. It meant nothing.

'Why don't I come for a swim with you? Show you exactly how I'm feeling,' he said. His lips traced the shell of her ear and a blast of heat whooshed through her. Rafe's body hard and uncompromising against hers. She imagined him slipping into the water. Pushing her up against the side of the pool. His muscular body slick against hers. The pleasure of it all. Touching her. Not stopping till she screamed his name.

But she needed to make some order of all this. The confused, jumbled kind of sensations he invoked. She slipped from his grasp. Pulled away. Gestured to his plate. 'Please, finish what you're eating. I may take a while to decide what I'm doing.'

He smiled, the warm indulgent tilt of his lips the same one that had greeted her on that couch in the mountains in front of a crackling fire, right before they'd kissed, and her world had tilted on its axis. She wasn't sure it would ever right again.

'Of course,' he said. 'I'll come and find you when I'm done.'

She turned her back and walked away, wishing she didn't want him to do so, all the while hoping that he made the wait worth it.

A run hadn't helped clear her head, not even jogging through the topiary garden, one of her favourite places in the vast palace grounds. In desperation she'd tried texting Sara but there'd been no response, the silence louder than words.

Lise's thoughts once again twisted and knotted, impossible to unravel. Guilt over her friend's loss. Confusion that Rafe might understand her because he'd been through punishing grief himself, but could she really trust him? She walked down the corridors of the palace towards the pool, bathing suit in hand. A swim, she'd do that now. And maybe he'd join her. A whisper of pleasure slithered through her at the thought. Treacherous body of hers. It knew what it wanted, and he was at the top of its wish list.

As she approached the competition-sized indoor pool, Albert stood near the doorway. She raised her eyebrows.

'I thought you'd like to know that the prime minister is here, talking to His Majesty.'

Lise frowned. There'd been no official appointments in her diary, this being her first morning back in the palace. Everything had been scheduled for the afternoon. Anyhow, she was the Queen. Shouldn't the prime minster be talking to her?

'Did Mr Hasselbeck say why?'

'He said the King would know what it was about. But His Majesty appeared…surprised.'

Albert was an astute judge of people, but she knew how fine an actor Rafe could be. The blood chilled in Lise's veins. There was no way anyone should circumvent her, and that was what was happening here. 'Where are they?'

'The study, Your Majesty.'

Her study. The other end of the palace. 'I think I should be there. How long have they been talking?'

Albert nodded. 'About fifteen minutes, give or take. Were you planning to change, and should I alert them to wait?'

She looked down at her clothes. If they couldn't handle a bit of spandex and sweat, then to hell with them. She took off at a jog. 'No, and no need to follow,' she shouted over her shoulder. Protocol be damned. There'd been more than enough secret chats about her in that study, with Rafe involved. No more.

As she ran through the corridors staff stopped, bowed, curtsied, stared. She tried to acknowledge them but had to be quick. Something was going on and she needed to find out what. It was the thing that had pricked her consciousness for a while now. There was a reason her father had demanded she marry Rafe. She didn't know why, but he'd wanted Rafe close.

As she approached the door to her study, she skidded to a halt. Took a few moments to catch her breath, check her hoodie was zipped up to a respectable level. Inside she heard Rafe's growl.

'How the hell did you let it come to this?'

She threw open the door. No knock, because she was Queen and there wasn't a door in this palace she had to knock on before entering. Two faces turned to her. The prime minister, who looked her up and down as if she had something nasty stuck to her shoe, and Rafe, whose gaze slid over her slowly, palpable as a caress. Hasselbeck stood. Rafe just sat there behind the desk, looking at her. His thunderous gaze softening to something no less stormy, but more heated.

Lise wanted to shout at them both, but she reined in her temper, barely.

'I would have thought, Prime Minister, that if you were calling on the palace, I should have been advised beforehand,' she said, trying to insert a chill into her voice commensurate with the ice permanently running through her veins. She eyed a red folder on the desk, open. Papers scattered across the dark desktop. Her desktop, behind which Rafe was sitting.

The usurper.

'My apologies, Your Majesty. There were a few matters I needed to discuss with His Majesty. I didn't wish to trouble you.'

Which likely meant he didn't think a woman could manage or understand what he was trying to say. He'd always dismissed her when she was a princess. She wouldn't stand for it, as Queen.

Though come to think of it, Hasselbeck looked decidedly sweaty. She didn't invite him to sit again, so he didn't. He glanced at Rafe, who said nothing, damn him. No rebuttal at all. Although he did have a slight smile on his face as if he was enjoying the scene. Of course, he should be standing too, and the lack of concern for propriety rankled her. But she'd deal with him later. She had her whole life to do so, as the cursed wedding ring on her finger perpetually reminded her.

'Did your conversation concern personal business with my husband, or business about Lauritania?' Hasselbeck fidgeted. She didn't need him to spell out the answer because, from his discomfort, she knew.

Lise wasn't the tallest of women, especially without heels. Still, she drew herself as tall as she could, given the circumstances.

'Anything that concerns my country, concerns me,' she hissed, but her eyes were on Rafe. He didn't have the good grace to look uncomfortable or chastened. He looked entertained. At least Hasselbeck appeared nervous, his neatly trimmed moustache quivering.

Rafe eased from the chair, then moved to the front of the desk. His eyes so dark they were almost black. He turned to the prime minister. 'Do you want to explain this, or shall I?'

Hasselbeck looked from one to the other then bowed. 'I'll leave you to discuss the situation, with my profound thanks.' He began to back away.

'You haven't been dismissed yet,' Rafe said.

The prime minister stopped at the door, eyes narrow and loathing written all over his face. He turned to Lise and the look on his face chastened a fraction.

'Ma'am?'

The request for permission mollified her only a little. 'You can go. But make sure this *never* happens again.'

The prime minister nodded, opened the door and fled. She knew the rotten scent of treachery when she smelled it, and it didn't leave the room with the prime minister. It stayed and clung to Rafe.

'You're glorious when you're magisterial,' he said. 'I think the man cowered.'

Rafe's voice was liquid heat. It was tempting to let it trickle through her and warm all her cold places, but she wouldn't let him distract her. Lise whipped around, the suppressed anger bubbling in her blood. Rafe didn't appear apologetic, and she hated that he stood in the room as if he'd always meant to be here.

'I'm the Queen. Over seven hundred years of history stand behind the role I now hold. You've been King for mere days. Why are you meeting the prime minister without me?'

Rafe didn't cower. He stood there all dark and brooding, his shirt stretched tight and far too distractingly over the muscles of his chest. He crossed his arms and his biceps bunched. Something heated slid inside her belly. Anger, that was all it was. Something to warm the frozen heart of her.

'His arrival was as much a surprise to me as it was to you.'

She clenched her jaw. The schemer in Rafe was coming through again. She didn't believe him, and she wouldn't be distracted by his brooding masculinity.

'I should have been called immediately.'

'I agree.' He raked a hand through his hair. Blew out a long, slow breath. 'Unfortunately, I became preoccupied with what he had to say.'

'Which was?'

'Did your father or brother ever discuss finance with you?'

'No,' she was forced to admit. She'd always been an afterthought if they'd thought of her at all. She'd formed the view long ago that if she wanted more, she had to make her own way. Even when she'd tried, it had to be attractive types of charities. Abandoned kittens and puppies because everybody thought they were cute and worth saving. Not the meatier issues of domestic abuse and homeless teenagers, which had been her true passion. Those she'd had to sneak around to see, in secret. Not any more.

Rafe ran a hand through his hair again, leaving it messy and dishevelled. 'You might want to take a seat.'

'I'm sure I've had worse news.' She'd never sit down to take bad news again, even if her knees trembled and her stomach churned. She was made of stronger stuff.

Rafe nodded. 'For some time, the country's fiscal position has been...precarious.'

He'd mentioned economics on their pretend honeymoon, then avoided the conversation. Everything in her stilled. 'How precarious?'

'The prime minister advised me that by the end of the year the government may not be able to pay the public service.'

She sank to a seat in spite of herself. This was something her father must have known of. Her mother, her brother too. How could she have been kept ignorant? Especially Rafe, when the perfect moment had arisen only days earlier. But then he hadn't wanted anything to ruin the perfect weekend of attempted seduction, had he?

'The government's plan includes support from me, provision of financial advice and a number of austerity measures.' He shuffled some papers, placed them into the red folder and handed it to her. 'It's all in here.'

She looked at him, leaning on the desk. One foot crossed over the other. The only thought swirling through her head was that he didn't seem surprised. At all.

'How long have you known?'

He hesitated, his mouth thinning to a taut line. He was thinking, and that told her all she needed. She'd bet the kingdom on him having known for—

'That the treasury has been in financial trouble? About five months.'

Bingo. He'd been told at about the time he'd begun seeking her out in earnest. At the time she'd thought he might be interested in her.

'That the economy's at risk of collapse,' Rafe added. 'About twenty minutes.'

The flame of humiliation and then hatred burned bright. She wasn't sure who she hated now, but since her father was dead and Rafe was here…

'My father offered you a princess, didn't he? To get your co-operation and assistance in digging Lauritania out of this mess.'

'Lise—'

'No. Stop right there.' She held up her hand. 'I *know*. My father needed your help, so he offered me as your reward.'

It was clear now. The desperation to get her to marry. The fury when she refused. Why couldn't her father have trusted her with the information? To save the country, she might have accepted the plan.

'Is that what you all saw in me?' she hissed, the pain of realisation too much to bear. She blinked away the hot sting of tears, 'A financial cost of doing business? Something to be traded?'

He cocked his head. Regarded her. Those dark eyes of his all-knowing.

'I saw a passionate young woman. A woman seeking permission to be herself.' His voice ran soft and silky across her skin. 'Something you should never have had to ask for.'

She hated that he knew so many of her secret desires, the old hurts. That he could read her so well. Even though she shouldn't think this way, he still called to her on some deep and hopeful level. That his seeming passion for her hadn't been faked. She crushed those sentiments. Stood, holding her head high.

'I'll take that report and read it. Decide how to manage the situation.'

'It gets worse.'

She stiffened her spine. She would not crumble. She wouldn't. 'How can it be *worse*?'

'Read the report, Lise.'

The betrayal stabbed deep. Her family dead, her country in ruins. She grabbed at her chest, unzipped her hoodie. She couldn't breathe.

'I'll need to assemble the best financial minds in the country—'

'I am the best financial mind in the country.'

It was said with no humility, but no hubris either. Still, Rafe was the last person that she wanted to talk to, even if he was the best at everything he did.

'I'd like a wider choice.'

He pushed away from the desk. 'It shouldn't be anyone who helped to cause the situation.'

She nodded. The suggestion seemed sensible, but she hated that he'd thought of it first. She picked up the red folder from the desktop then headed for the door.

'Remember, Lise. You don't have to do things alone. I'm—'

'What?' She whipped round, gripping the folder tight in her hands. 'Here to help? Or the truth, here to keep more secrets? Because that's what everyone's been doing. Hiding things. And why wouldn't they? I'm the Queen nobody wanted.'

'Do you really believe you're so hard to love?'

She turned and left the room without answering, the question still spitting like a vicious cat in her ears. Because the answer was clear. People only loved what she represented. No one had ever truly loved her.

Rafe sliced through the cool water, pushing harder and faster till his muscles screamed. He'd been a fool not to call for Lise immediately. He'd allowed his own arrogance to ignore the obvious, that she would see the meeting with the prime minister as another betrayal. Whatever fragile trust he'd been hoping to build, it had been smashed in one morning.

He hauled himself out from the edge of the pool, chest heaving from fifty brutal laps to burn through his fury. Fury that he wasn't in the water with Lise right now, fury at himself because the perfect opportunity to discuss this had arisen on their weekend away and he'd selfishly kept the truth hidden. But most of all, fury towards a prime minister who should have briefed his Queen. That man was one to watch, and carefully. He'd seen Hasselbeck's spark at Lise's cold rage. Fear for his own job no doubt, but a silent glee with her anger at Rafe as well.

Rafe knew the government didn't rate her, and they barely tolerated him. He scrubbed a towel through his hair. Rough-dried the rest of his body then lashed the towel around his waist. The lot of them were vermin. Rats who'd grown fat whilst the country suffered. It had all worked well with a complacent, lazy king. Lise was an unknown, and people knew his reputation too well. If they worked together, the things he and Lise could achieve were mind-boggling. One crack, and people would try to tear them apart. He refused to accept that. He'd be written into the history books as the commoner King who saved the nation. *Everyone* would know his name. He'd accept nothing less.

His phone rang from the table he'd tossed it on before diving into the water. He snatched it and swiped to answer before checking who'd called.

'Yes!'

'Hello to you too, Your Majesty.' Lance's amused voice clipped at him. 'I'm guessing married life is going swimmingly?'

Rafe took a slow breath. His friend was one of the few people with whom he could be completely honest, however even this was a stretch. He went with the anger still crackling through him.

'Why the hell are you calling so soon after my wedding?'

'Why are you answering?' Lance chuckled. 'Haven't you got better things to be doing? That beautiful wife of yours, for starters.'

Regaining broken trust, though he'd never tell Lance, even if the man was his best friend.

'What do you want?'

'I've a favour to ask in person. It's a delicate situation.'

Rafe pinched the bridge of his nose. The universe conspired against him. Still, if his friend needed a favour Rafe would always answer the call. One thing he and Lance had promised each other all those years ago whilst at school was that when one of them asked for assistance, the other would honour the request. Neither of them had failed their boyhood promise yet. He wouldn't be the one to start.

'When do you want to meet?'

'Tonight. Around eight.'

'I'll arrange it with Security. We can have dinner.'

'Thank you, my friend. I promise that I won't intrude on your wedded bliss for too long.'

'You'd better not,' Rafe growled, and disconnected the phone to Lance's laughter.

He took another deep breath to tamp the anger down before walking out of the swimming pavilion, through the palace and towards his rooms, the marble floors cold beneath his feet. He didn't care that he was half dressed, didn't give a damn about propriety. He needed to find Lise and start the dialogue to regain her trust.

As he passed one of the hundreds of anonymous doorways in the place, he saw her. Pacing across a conservatory overlooking a perfectly sculpted topiary garden. In her hands she held the red folder, flicking through it with restless energy. Dressed not in the exercise clothes that lovingly covered every inch of her exquisite body, leaving nothing to the imagination. Driving him close to distraction, which had meant he couldn't stand when she'd burst into the room but had remain seated to get his body under control lest he disgrace himself. No, now she paced in a demure, high-necked, long-sleeved black dress. Once again steeped in the colour of mourning, a deep frown marring her brow. She seemed so pale and fragile, trying to absorb the news. Without thinking, he stepped into the room.

Lise whipped around at his approach, wide-eyed with surprise. She looked at him, over his torso, down his body. It wasn't a cursory survey either. Her eyes snagging on his chest, lingering on his abdomen, finally hitching on the knot of his towel. He walked slowly towards her, because she seemed as skittish as the deer who inhabited the wilder mountain regions here. Ready to run at the first sight of trouble.

'What are you doing dressed like that?' Her voice was a soft rasp against his skin.

He shrugged. 'I've been swimming.'

'Could you not have…?' She flapped her hand about in front of her. She wasn't looking at him now. Her eyes were everywhere else. The bloom of red creeping up her throat.

'What?' he asked. Knowing exactly what. Despite all her righteous anger, he affected her, and desire was something he could work with.

'Nothing.' She held her head high in glorious defiance of everything he knew she still felt for him. Passion such as they'd experienced didn't die easily and sometimes anger only inflamed it.

An addictive thought.

He turned his mind to something more mundane before his own desire for her became apparent. 'Lance will be visiting tonight, around eight.'

Something whispered across her face. Her eyes widened a fraction. She chewed at the side of her bottom lip. 'It's nice to have a friend. Say hello to him for me.'

'You're welcome to join us.'

She shook her head. 'I need an early night.'

What they needed was to be in bed together. Burning away the emotion and fury with their bodies. Not this cold war.

He nodded to the folder she held before her. The red clutched against her chest like a garish wound. 'Have you finished reading?'

He'd been given a summary and could only guess the horrors it contained.

She dropped her head. The knuckles on her hands gripping the folder whitened. 'They want to rationalise the public service.'

This he knew. A gross suggestion that punished the innocent whilst those responsible still grew fat, rewarded by their own negligence.

'Sacking twenty thousand. As a start,' she whispered, then her voice firmed, 'I'll sell the Crown jewels before I destroy the lives of twenty thousand people.'

'You can't do that. The country needs its symbols.'

She raised her chin, looking every bit the monarch she'd been crowned. He wished her people could see her like this. Then they wouldn't doubt her, they'd exalt her.

'People can't eat diamonds and those precious symbols won't keep them warm in the coming winter.'

'We'll find another way.' He only hoped the alternative was better. It had to be. She seemed unmoved.

'How long will it take to assemble a meeting of experts to discuss this?'

'I've already given some acceptable candidates some thought. Hopefully only a few days, considering the urgency.'

She pulled herself upright, her mouth tight and hard as she stared him down.

'Then make it so.' He might have smiled at the very words he'd used with her only hours earlier being tossed back at him, as if he were one of her minions. But he didn't think she'd appreciate any mirth. Not now. She tapped the folder in her arms. 'I'll spend the evening considering this. I don't want to be disturbed.'

She stalked from the room. Damn it all. He hadn't improved anything. Rafe watched her leave, the click of her low heels echoing on the marble floors.

They were now further away from each other than ever.

CHAPTER EIGHT

LISE SAT ON the couch in her room, the cursed red folder on the table in front of her. A barely touched dinner to her side. She took a deep shuddering breath, but the trembling wouldn't stop. She was cold, so cold. How could no one have told her? What were they thinking, that they could hide the coming disaster? She buried her face in her quivering hands. Pressed her fingers hard into her eyes, trying to push back the tears that stung her eyelids. If only her family had confided in her. She might have married Rafe if the importance of their union had been disclosed. She could have helped save the country in that way. Then her family would have lived. All ifs, buts and maybes.

She stood and looked out onto the darkening valley. The lights of the capital blinking on as dusk fell. All those people out there, living their lives. Hoping, dreaming and her government was demanding she decimate them. No. Never.

But she didn't know what to do. Everything in that cursed report sounded so urgent. Budget emergencies led by poor decisions and some even poorer speculative investment of Lauritania's funds, and here they were. The country's fate was in her hands, yet none of them trusted her with it. Her actions would affect thousands. In her time at finishing school, with the palace tutors, managing a country's economy had never figured in her education. She hadn't even known how to manage a bank account until Albert taught her, a life skill he'd said every person needed to learn. She'd been locked in a pretty tower, given nothing to help her negotiate life other than being told she'd have an auspicious marriage and her husband would look after everything from then on.

The ache welled in her chest. Gripped her throat till she couldn't breathe. She clutched the back of a chair. Weeks of fighting to hold onto control and it came to this. People who didn't even know it yet were relying on her to make the right decisions. Twenty *thousand* people. She fought the first sob that tore from her throat, the tears that flowed freely down her cheeks for the first time since she'd been told of her family's deaths, but she couldn't hold it in any longer. If no one trusted her, how could she *fix* things? It broke out with a rush, the grief, the fear. An avalanche she couldn't hold back. Sobbing in a way she wasn't sure would ever stop.

The door adjoining creaked open. A cool rush of air flooded in from Rafe's rooms. She straightened, wiped frantically at her eyes and nose but there was no hiding these tears as she tried to choke down the agony cutting her in two. As the whole atmosphere of the room changed, she knew without looking that he was now bearing down on her.

'Leave me alone.' Her voice scratched out too rough and raw to hide how she'd weakened. She turned her back so he couldn't see, shoulders hunched over, wanting to curl into herself and disappear.

'Lise, I heard you.' That voice. So soft, so gentle. Wrapping around her like a goose-down comforter. She sensed the warmth of him, standing behind her. For a moment she imagined he could take it all away. The pain, the fear. If only she could lean in, accept some support. She wouldn't need long. Warm herself from all the cold...

No.

Her parents and her brother were lying dead in the family crypt. They'd never be warm again and neither should she be. She wouldn't succumb to this, or to a man who made a career of temptation. And like everyone else, he mistrusted her. If he didn't, he would have told her everything when he'd had his chance.

She whipped around, chewing at the inside of her mouth to stop her lips trembling. Pointing to the door between their rooms. 'Out!'

Rafe stood there unmoving. Dressed in a perfectly pressed business shirt and trousers. Black hair raked back. Dark, brooding features. Looking for all the world like the King he'd become by their marriage. Yet what she hated most, more than seeing the man she'd married looking as if this were the role he was born to, was the tenderness in his eyes. They promised things she could never accept.

'You're crying. Let me—'

'No.' No one should see her weakness. Certainly not him.

'Lise. I keep telling you, you're not alone.' That deep, low voice was a soft burr against her skin. She ignored it. In truth, she *was* alone. Sara wasn't responding to her texts and Rafe…her emotions were too tangled to know how to deal with him. Instead, she raised her head high. Another tear escaped, sliding down her cheek. She scrubbed it away.

'I asked you to leave. Will none of my subjects actually obey me?'

Rafe held up his hands in mock surrender. 'I've never been known for my obedience.'

It had been the one flaw in her plan for this marriage. A belief he'd listen to and accept what she'd demanded. An error of judgement born of desperation to carry out her father's final wishes and assuage her guilt.

'I wish I'd married someone who was.'

He crossed his arms. His biceps bunched under the fabric in an all too tantalising way. Reminding her of what he'd looked like with his shirt off this morning. His arms, beautifully defined. His chest, the smattering of hair coalescing in a dark line bisecting the ridges of his abdomen and disappearing below the towel. Wrapped around those narrow hips. Water sparkling on his skin like diamonds. She dragged her eyes from the belt around the waist of his trousers. Tried to look at his face instead.

'You'd better get used to it,' he said. 'I'm with you until death. It's a promise I intend to keep.'

She glared at him. That reminder etched for ever into the inside of her wedding band. 'I'm the Queen, I'm sure I can arrange an execution if I put my mind to it.'

'Happily for me, capital punishment was abolished by the constitutional amendment of—'

She threw up her hands. 'Don't talk to me about my own constitution! What good is being Queen if you can't take the head of someone who's annoying you?' His beautiful lips curved into a sensual smile. It peeved her that he wasn't in the slightest bit concerned about her threats, hollow though they were. 'Why aren't you more afraid of me?'

'I've told you before, you're magnificent when you're being magisterial.' His eyes were dark and sultry in his handsome face. He began to stroll towards her. 'Irresistible, in fact.'

She moved, placing an armchair between her and him, but that didn't seem to offer protection. His steps were languid, almost careless, but that heated gaze of his was fixed on her.

'Lance will be here soon,' she said. Rafe stepped around some furniture and her stomach flipped as if it were filled with a flock of swallows that roosted in the palace ramparts. Every part of her skin too tight in her clothes. She scratched at the high neck of her dress. Her body melting and softening as he bore down on her.

Rafe checked his watch. 'He can wait.'

Worst of it all, she still wanted him. Craved the man who was edging closer, backing her into a corner from which she didn't want to escape. She glanced at her bed. So tempting for him to tumble her on it, thrust his hands into her hair, hold her tight and kiss her again. Let him bury himself in her and subdue her fears with cries of pleasure. But she'd made a promise to herself. She was worth nothing if she couldn't uphold it.

'I—I'll have you locked in…in the dungeons.'

His smile was pure predator. Oh, how she wanted to succumb. Let herself be devoured. He was in front of the chair now, a single step around it and he'd be right there. He raised an arrogant eyebrow. One touch and she wasn't sure she'd say no to him.

'I don't believe the palace has any,' Rafe said with a smile.

On a delicate table next to her bed sat the internal palace phone. She nodded towards it. 'All I need to do is to press the duress button. You'll find out about the dungeons soon after.'

'If that's what you need to protect you from yourself.' Rafe gave a deep, mocking kind of laugh. 'You're afraid of your feelings. And with me, there's nowhere for you to hide.'

She stopped her retreat. Firmed her spine and stood tall in the face of his taunts.

'There are *no* feelings where you're concerned.'

A muscle in the side of his jaw twitched as he took another step towards her, close enough now to touch. 'Prove it.' His voice was smooth and hard. Silk over steel. 'Kiss me, then make that claim again.'

Recollections of their *only* kiss burst into her consciousness like a firework. Heat crackled over her, but she wouldn't back down, not whilst he stood there and mocked her. She closed the gap between them. Cupped her hands to the warm skin of his jaw and pulled him down to her. His lips parted, his breath hot as he brushed his lips against hers and the thrill of that soft touch rushed to her core. Their mouths fused as he slid his arms round her and dragged her body against his, no space between them as he angled his head and their tongues touched. Twined together.

She speared her fingers into his hair and gripped, whether to pull him down closer or push him away, she wasn't sure. It was as if her world exploded in a conflagration of need and panting breaths that caused her heart to race and turned her core molten. This was more than a kiss; it was a battle of desire and erotic promise. She trembled as he pressed her to him, the evidence of his arousal bold and impossible to miss.

Lise was lost in sensation. His hair caught in her fingers, his mouth moving over hers. Their bodies, melding together. She flexed against his hardness and there was a groan. Her? Him? She couldn't be sure. Then he stopped and pulled his mouth away. Looking down on her, his eyes fierce as she let him go. He stood back. Lips still parted. Breaths heaving like her own. She craved to be in his arms again, fused together with no distance between them. Proving that not only was she craven, but a liar as well. Except in this moment, only a step from her, Rafe was as far away as he'd ever been.

He glanced over her shoulder towards the door of her room, his gaze distant. Then he frowned and turned his attention to her once more. Eyes glittering in the low light of the evening.

'Anything to say, Lise?' His lips curled into a wicked smirk, but she didn't react. Trying to give nothing away when everything inside her seethed with emotion. 'Because that felt a *lot* like feelings to me.'

She attempted to ignore his look of triumph, as Rafe brushed past her and strode from the room.

Rafe throttled the neck of a dusty wine bottle as he stalked around the bowels of the castle. He'd ostensibly come to find the palace cellars to select a vintage for dinner, but in truth he couldn't face Lance, not with anger and unrequited desire still careering out of control through his blood. He needed to regain his famed control, which was rapidly shredding because of a kiss, which once again proved Lise was not the Ice Queen she pretended to be, but a woman on fire.

What kind of monster did she think he was, leaving her to cry? And it had been more than simple tears. The agony of the sounds had had him rushing through the door between their rooms before he could even give what he was doing much thought. The brokenness of it all. Perhaps he should have backed away, but he was never a man to be shy and she'd needed *someone* to comfort her, even though Lise was desperate to run from herself.

He checked his watch, realising that in his introspection he'd forgotten the time. Taking stock of his surroundings, he found himself in a cavernous storage area, piled with all kinds of forgotten treasures. An ostentatious statue of Bacchus stood in the corner and the gleam of burnished wood and gilding peeked from under dust covers. He turned at the sound of footsteps.

'Where are you?' That male voice. The clipped British accent. 'Ah. Store Two. This looks interesting.'

'Lance.'

His friend strolled through the doorway, holding a glass half full of red wine. He looked around the space, eyes narrowing to settle on the bronze in the corner. 'That is the ghastliest statue. I've a client who'd love it. Do you think the Queen would sell?'

As he'd journeyed through the lower reaches of the palace Rafe had seen corners stuffed with discarded objects. The palace itself was full of them, rooms shut off and never used.

'She might. I could talk to her.' Lance had an eye for quality and was one of the finest antique experts in Europe. He'd know what was worth something and perhaps they could divest themselves of some of the unwanted treasures gathering dust.

'I'm not sure that'll go well.' Lance snorted. 'What are you doing down here? In the doghouse already after four days of marriage? That's a stellar achievement. I don't believe even I'd have done better.'

'I was getting wine for dinner.' Rafe gestured to the bottle.

'As you can see, I already have some.' Lance held his glass to the light, which shimmered through the ruby liquid, then took a hefty swig. 'This is a lovely drop. The Queen was most gracious when we couldn't find you. She asked staff to check your suite. Strange to have your own rooms considering you're married...'

Lance was many things, and thirsty for information was one. He didn't peddle in it, necessarily, but had a rampant curiosity. Rafe wouldn't give him any more to pique his interest, or he'd never hear the end of it because his friend had always liked to bring him crashing back to earth.

'That's the way it's done in the palace.'

Lance cocked his head. 'If that's the story you want to tell.'

'What other story would there be?' His voice sounded distant, unconvincing. Swallowing down the lies to his best friend was more difficult than he thought.

'Whilst considering whether to mount a search party Lise and I had a lovely chat. She mentioned Carl, like she didn't believe he was real.' Rafe's heart stopped for one beat, then picked up its pace.

A sharp ache and then anger, stoked inside. Even though he'd bared his soul to Lise, she thought it was an untruth? Rafe didn't know why that realisation knifed him deep inside.

Anyhow, Carl's name shouldn't be mentioned in random fashion. His memory should be carefully handled, with respect.

'I assured her that, whilst you might be a cad, you weren't known for lying,' Lance said. 'Not about that, at least.'

Rafe tried to sound disinterested. 'Thank you for your support.'

'You haven't spoken about him in years.' Lance's eyes narrowed.

'Did you tell Her Majesty that as well?'

'That's for you to divulge.' He looked sharp as a hawk. The pause went on for a few seconds too long. No doubt he was waiting for Rafe to fill it. Rafe stayed silent. 'Though, speaking of cads, *I've* never been relegated to a palace storeroom.'

Rafe looked at the rough-hewn ceiling and thanked the change of topic.

'As I said, I was finding wine for our dinner.'

Lance raised an imperious eyebrow. 'Hmm. The palace has a cellarmaster for that sort of thing. The staff are intrigued. I believe I heard something about…dungeons. There are all kinds of whispers going on upstairs.'

Which was what Rafe hadn't wanted. He

thought he'd seen a shadow under the door of Lise's room just before he'd left. People were watching and listening to them, of that he was certain. 'There's nothing to be intrigued about. Lise is playing her own game.'

'Is this one of those grown-up games like doctors and nurses? Or should I say, jailer and captive?' Lance's mouth twisted into a wicked smirk. 'Though I would have thought being the jailer was more *your* style. Of course, for an exquisite young woman like Lise, I can see why exceptions could be made. She really is delicious company. Even I—'

'Lance. Enough.' Rafe's voice was a low hiss. He stormed towards his friend and Lance threw back his head, roaring with laughter.

'How the mighty has fallen.' He raised his glass in a mocking toast. 'Drop the jealous husband act. You've always had your life so carefully planned, pardon me if I'm not entertained by this turn of events.'

'You know my thoughts on love.'

'I wasn't talking about love, were you?' Lance cocked his head. 'How quaint.'

'Remind me, why are you still in the country and how can I have you deported?'

'You're King. Call Security.'

'I expected you to escape after the reception, being allergic to weddings as you are.'

Lance began peering under dust covers. 'I've been checking out the wildlife. It's most distracting.'

That was the friend he knew. Lance loved women and women loved Lance, only none of them could pin him down. 'You had something sensitive to discuss.'

'Yes. Down to business.' He slipped a piece of paper from the inner pocket of his suit jacket. 'Someone wants to leave the country and can't access their passport.'

Rafe raised his eyebrows and leaned forwards. 'What are you up to and is it legal?'

'Looking out for your interests, and it's perfectly legal. You have enemies.'

'I had enemies at school.' Rafe snorted. 'They're still there, the same bullies. What's new?'

Lance looked serious, a state of being Rafe knew his friend tried to avoid although he was a serious man deep down. His friend might have carefully cultivated the image of a rich and lazy dilettante. He was none of those things.

'They're consolidating. The Queen's an unknown. People are taking sides.'

A chill ran through him. Rafe had suspected as much, though the thought that people were choosing sides already was concerning. There was a lot to do to save the economy. He needed cooperation, not frustration.

'The little bird I'm helping doesn't want to be

used as a pawn in someone's game. If you sign this form, I'll have a replacement passport tomorrow and we'll be gone.'

'Why didn't you ask Her Majesty, since she's such a fine new friend?'

Lance handed Rafe the paper. Rafe looked at the name. Raised his eyebrows. 'Sara Conrad?'

He shouldn't be surprised. The Crown Prince had kept mistresses, even during his engagement. It was a well-kept secret, but Rafe had a way of finding these things out because knowledge was power. He wondered now whether Sara had ever loved Ferdinand, contrary to Lise's romantic delusions about her brother's relationship with her friend.

'Now you know why I didn't ask Lise. I'll leave her to her grief, uninterrupted.'

Rafe agreed. Lise was so mired in her own sadness she mightn't understand others moving on. 'You and Sara?'

His friend had a reputation, which he upheld with impunity. When younger, Rafe had tried to keep up, until he'd realised it was a fruitless endeavour. Lance took things to an entirely different level.

'You know how aristocrats do things. She fears plans are afoot to marry her off again.' Aah. That was why Lance had helped her... The sour taint of bile rose in Rafe's throat. No matter the truth of

Sara and Ferdinand's relationship, a woman's fiancé had only recently been placed in the ground. That she'd be married off again disgusted him. 'People are trying to create new allegiances. I'm helping a damsel in distress and thwarting an attempt at a power block.'

Rafe rubbed his hands over his face. Their argument in Lise's suite, the shadows at the door. If their enemies thought there were cracks, they would hammer deeper wedges into them.

'Have you a pen?'

Lance whipped one from his pocket. Rafe took it, scrawled his signature on the page and handed it back.

'Thank you, my friend. Do you need me to leave so you can make peace with Lise?' Lance downed the last of his wine and clapped Rafe on the back. 'I've heard making up is half the fun of a fight.'

Rafe shook his head. 'Dinner's waiting and I refuse to disappoint the chef.' Even more importantly, he wanted to hear more about the 'whispers' Lance claimed to overhear. Time for Lise, later. He'd eat some food, tamp down his anger. Let Lise think she'd won for tonight. But tomorrow? He was having a conversation with his wife.

CHAPTER NINE

Rafe strode from the dining room back towards Lise's suite. He'd wanted to talk over the calm of breakfast, where she couldn't hide. Yet she hadn't been in the dining room this morning. She'd been breakfasting in her own room, so the staff told him.

In bed.

It seemed an age ago when he'd made that suggestion to her, hardly crediting it was only yesterday. How life could change in twenty-four hours. He should be there with her right now. They could be feasting on each other as he'd intended, rather than sitting down to the luxurious breakfast he'd had, which tasted little better than sawdust on his tongue. A poor substitute when all he craved to taste was her. The fire of anger burned a little too brightly in his gut as he made his way to their rooms. More at himself than anything else. He had greater finesse than this, and yet around her all his plans and good intentions crumbled to nothing.

Breakfast in bed.

They both knew what he'd meant. Lise's pupils had flared wide and dark when he'd mentioned it.

Her lips parted, breaths quick and shallow. She'd wanted him as much as he did her. Arousal joined the irritation hammering at his cold, calculated self-control, the two fresh emotions now a heady and dangerous mix that had him thrumming, not at all conducive to polite conversation.

In other circumstances they could have burned it away together. Not now. He reached her bedroom door and knocked. Perhaps a little too firmly. Took a breath to calm the driving pulse beating low and hard.

'Come in.' Even though her voice was muffled slightly by the wood, it was firm and clear. She should be worried. Perhaps she hadn't seen the scurrilous online gossip in the tabloids yet? He thrust open the door and entered.

Lise stood near the window, framed by the view behind of the lake and capital she now ruled. Looking as regal as any monarch he'd ever met, with her chin held high and spine stiff. She wasn't the tallest of women, but in that pose it still seemed as if she looked down at him. That she appeared entirely unaffected irritated and enthralled him in equal measure. He wanted to break through that cool veneer. Like before, marvelling at the passionate treasure underneath after he'd stripped her back to her truest self.

Rafe strolled into the room trying to appear nonchalant when every part of him stretched taut, primed for the spears of battle. Even today, she wore black. A dress of some sort, high-necked, below the knee. Belted at her slender waist. Skimming over the swell of her breasts, the curve of her hip. Yet it could have been the sheerest lingerie, the way the impeccable fit called to him. He barely understood this need. How his craving for power, establishing his legacy, was being overborne by another craving... For her.

'Sleep well, Lise?'

She glanced at the unmade bed. A tray still there, with food half eaten. Visions flickered through his head like a stuttering film reel. Lise, naked and glowing in the soft light of a fire. Body arched and gasping as he tasted her. Head thrown back as she came. The breathless whispers as her fingers gripped his hair. *Rafe, Rafe...*

And that beat deep inside took up a relentless pace, riding him hard. His famed control fled where she was concerned. Yet she seemed entirely unmoved, though her gaze didn't leave him, following every footstep as he moved closer to her. A polite distance, but still close enough to see her throat convulse as she swallowed.

'Yes, I did. And I can highly commend your suggestion of breakfast in bed. An inspired idea.' She sauntered towards that bed with a taunting sway of her hips. Picked up a piece of bread slathered with jam and bit into it. Consuming the morsel slowly, licking a stray crumb from her lips once finished. Minx. 'Did you sleep well too?'

'As I've said before, I'm not afflicted by poor sleep.' Although his night had been plagued by dreams of being buried in the wet heat of her body. Wasted fantasies when they should have been playing them out together.

Lise raised a supercilious brow. He'd seen that look before, proving she was her father's daughter in some ways at least. 'Your clear, unblemished conscience.'

No, she was not doing this. He had nothing to feel guilty for. He raised a brow to match hers. Time to end what he'd started the night before.

'I never took you for a coward.'

She turned her back on him to stare out of the window. 'I'm not, I'm—'

'Which is why you threatened to call Security and have me locked in a dungeon.' No more lies. It stopped today.

Lise whipped around. 'I told you to go. You don't listen.'

'I do—'

'You're no better than the rest of them!' She stabbed the air in front of her with her finger. *'"What's the point competing in the downhill championships since you can't win?" "Why learn about running the country when you won't*

*need to?" "Who cares about your thoughts on
the subject since you must marry?"'*

The words had taken on a mocking tone. She
shook her head, then looked directly at him, her
gaze cold and piercing. '"*When you claim you
want me to leave, you really mean stay.*" No,
Rafe. You might hear what I say, but you don't
listen to what I want.'

Her wrenching sobs from the evening before
still rang in his ears. Not a sound he would easily
forget. 'I will not ignore another person in distress, especially not the woman I married. How
many times do I have to tell you, you don't need
to do this alone?'

She looked down at her twisting fingers then
seemed to check herself, grasping onto the back
of a chair instead. Her fingertips blanched white.
'I don't deserve any sympathy.'

Rafe didn't understand. If she wasn't deserving now, when would she ever be? He moved towards her. Slowed his breathing. Tried to gentle
his voice. 'You needed my support. I understand
you're afraid—'

'Your arrogance is astonishing.' Her eyes narrowed. 'You know *nothing*.'

Oh, no. This, he would not accept. He'd trans-
formed his family's humble though successful
business into a billion-dollar empire. Perhaps she
needed reminding of how much this country *owed*

him. And he'd take it, in the end. It was all his due. People would *never* forget the De Villiers name.

'My arrogance, as you call it, is well placed.' His jaw clenched, the taunts from the Kings' Academy searing into his consciousness. Leeches of the aristocracy were prepared to take what he offered when they were at risk of losing everything. His money to save their skins. Particularly those families whose sons had disparaged him at school. Who had bullied Carl till he'd left. 'The De Villiers group props up most of Lauritania's oldest companies, almost destroyed by complacency and lack of government support. There's nothing made here that you eat or drink or wear that doesn't have my name behind it. So, say again that you don't need me, and I'll walk from this room right now.'

He'd taken a risk, calculated but a risk, nonetheless. She said nothing, which was telling, and a small victory. The country needed him, but he wanted her to admit that *she* needed him too. The continued silence made him grit his teeth till he would be silent no more.

'As I thought, you can't. Now, for last night…' He took a slow breath, trying to tamp down the growing maelstrom inside. Perhaps it wasn't the best time to have this conversation, with both of them on edge. But he was never one to run away from a fight. 'To the rest of the world, we must be seen as one. An unassailable force. Nothing less is acceptable.'

In truth, nothing else would save the country.

Lise hadn't moved, her face unreadable except for the tug at her lower lip as she worried her teeth over it.

'To whom is it unacceptable? The one who concentrates daily on the *narrative* in the papers?' She lifted her chin at him. 'You know what I see when I look at you? A man absorbed by self-interest.'

He refused to acknowledge the prickle at the base of his skull. Something like a conscience. No, he wouldn't allow that to go unanswered. Rafe shook his head. 'You look at me and you're terrified of your feelings.'

'Is that so? When you look at *me*, Rafe, what do you see?' She waved her hands up and down her body. 'The Princess I was or the Queen I've become? Or is it the woman who told her father in their last argument that she wouldn't cry if he died? That her family could go to hell? That I renounced all claims to the Crown?'

Rafe stilled, as if someone had frozen him solid on the spot. She'd renounced her line in succession to avoid marrying him? She wanted him *that* little? The chill of her admission invaded him to the core. 'Did anyone else hear you say it?'

Lise's lip curled to a sneer. 'Oh, don't worry,

Rafe. As you know, under our constitution I must sign a formal acknowledgement of renunciation. I can't lose my job simply because I say I don't like it any more. Quitting's not that easy. Your position as King is safe.'

She misunderstood his intentions. Any hint of destabilisation now would be disastrous. This argument had to be defused and yet they were both itching for a fight, the air electric between them. He shook his head. 'That's not what I meant.'

She threw up her hands. 'Why doesn't anyone say what they mean?'

Lise wanted honesty; he'd give it to her.

'It's difficult because honesty has been used as a weapon against me.' Rafe took a slow breath. 'For example, there's a reason I don't talk about Carl. When I tried after his death, his memory was used to taunt me by boys at school. The only time I've spoken about him to anyone other than my family or Lance was to you.'

Lise's eyes widened. 'Do you think *I'm* going to hurt you like that?'

He didn't respond because his answer might give her even more ammunition against him. She knew more ways than most to damage him if she thought about it hard enough.

'What I'm trying to explain is that we all say terrible things, and especially to our parents. Things designed to hurt that we don't mean. You think when Carl died, I didn't blame my mother and father for sending us to that school? Had your parents lived, they would have forgiven you as mine did. It's what families do.'

'If they love you, yes.'

Lise chewed on her bottom lip, the look on her face lost and broken. He didn't know how to respond because he suspected she was right.

'We need to stop fighting amongst ourselves. Those in power await your missteps. You offended their aristocratic pride by choosing me over one of their own. They'll punish you for it.'

She raised her chin, her gaze cool and magnificent as the snow-capped mountains that surrounded them. 'Let them try.'

'They already are.' Her eyes widened a fraction. Staff were talking about last night, as Lance had suggested. Salacious snippets for the press. Most, outrageous, but the hints of truth were there. Enough to have people questioning what was going on in the royal bedroom. 'Check this morning's Internet gossip pages if you don't believe me. None of that is good for the country.'

Lise hesitated a moment, then nodded.

'You're right. We're at cross purposes and the country's running out of time. But I have requirements of my own…' He stepped forward, opened his mouth to try and convince her once again that he was on her side. She held up her hand in a stop motion and the words died. 'No more secrets.'

'Agreed. I'm your greatest supporter in this place.'

Lise continued to stare him down.

'Then prove it.'

Rafe had been right. She hated it, railed against it, but couldn't dismiss his good judgement. The more reputable papers kept a dignified silence on the subject, but the tabloids had been full of titillating stories about their relationship. Even she could admit some of the headlines were quite clever. Things like, *Who's the King of the Castle?* Or Albert's particular favourite, *Dungeons and Dragon Queen*. She pored over each one, assessing the damage to the Crown over the days since. It terrified her, the way the stories took on a life of their own. Small truths turning into giant fictions.

The sourness of bile rose in her throat. All at the knowledge this was self-inflicted. She and Rafe tried to make up the lost ground. Out amongst the thankfully adoring public where everyone was all warm greetings and not entirely worried smiles. There, at least, they worked as a team. In private too, there had been a small thaw and, she had to admit, this way was easier. Seeing again the man she'd admired once. The one who had made her feel as if anything was possible. But there had been no more meaningful touches. No touching at all. Rafe had been kind, attentive. Respectful and distant in a way. And each time he was close, she *wanted*.

Her head still told her he was wrong for her. Her body cried he was wrong in all the right ways. It drove her mad. The churn of anxiety in her belly mixed with the curl of desire. Swirling and twisting her into tighter knots. She craved like a drug the sweet oblivion his body could provide. The floating bliss. The forgetting. During the day she could throw herself into duty. Meeting her people, hearing their concerns, and even solving some of them. She'd begun to enjoy that sense of achievement when once she'd believed there was nothing about the role she'd wanted or could much contribute to. Then at night Rafe invaded her dreams, till she woke all slick and wet with his name gasped from her lips.

There was no off switch to this need. It simmered barely below boiling point, overflowing when she least expected. Even today, as they worked to save the country with him commanding the room. A picture of rakish perfection in his bespoke suit. His hair curling in that careless kind of way that tempted her to reach out and sink her hands into the midnight darkness of it. Brush it away from his forehead when the unruly strands fell—

'Your Majesty?'

She snapped herself from the daydream. Realised she'd been staring at him. The corners of his mouth tilted in a soft, knowing smile and her heart tripped a beat. Now a room full of eminent financial experts waited on her next words. Sworn to maintain confidentiality about the true state of Lauritania's economy until some credible solutions could be seized upon in the hope of solving the country's woes. They'd spent the day working through options, and here she was fantasising.

'I suggest cutting parliamentary travel entitlements,' she said, though it would cause a riot amongst parliamentarians. 'Flying first class is a luxury they can forgo.'

Lise stifled a yawn, her eyes watering as she did. She needed coffee and a moment to herself. One where she might breathe without the weight of expectation crushing her. 'Ladies and gentlemen, perhaps we could take a break. I'm sure everyone would like some time to stretch their legs, check their phones. We can get back to saving the country in twenty minutes. Some refreshments will be served outside.'

There was murmur of assent. People bowed or curtsied as they left through open glass doors onto a secluded patio, leaving her blissfully alone. She turned away from the garden view, to look at an imposing portrait on the wall. The past few days being watched over by a painting of Lauritania's last and greatest Queen, Marie. Was it a deliberate decision to use this room? In the palace, rarely did anything happen by coincidence. Lise stared up at her great-great-grandmother, dressed in an exquisite, bejewelled gown. A monarch who'd ruled the country successfully for over seventy years. What advice would the woman have for Lise now, when her parents had given her none?

'You look like her.'

The soft burr of Rafe's voice whispered over her. She hadn't heard him come into the room again, but he was close. The awareness of how near he stood shimmered down her spine.

She studied the Queen's portrait. Marie's expression distant, serene.

'Which part?'

'Her eyes.' The same blue as her own, so lifelike it was as if they looked straight into the heart of her, almost like a judgement. A reminder to Lise that she must not fail here. Rafe moved to her side. 'There's a steel in them.'

'Me? Steely?' She shook her head. 'No.'

He clasped his hands behind his back. 'You've never been on the receiving end of your wrath.'

'Neither have you.'

'When you threatened to take my head or lock me in the dungeon—' he raised a knowing brow and placed his hand to his chest '—I feared for my very existence.'

He seemed so earnest, yet his eyes glittered wickedly. She laughed. 'I don't believe that for a moment.'

Rafe turned to look at Marie's portrait again, his gaze lost in it. 'You might be surprised.'

'What do you fear?'

His attention left the painting, all of it now directed at her as if peering deep into her soul. It was an uncomfortable sensation. The corner of his mouth kicked up, 'Queen Marie has never been forgotten, and neither will you.'

There seemed to be such honesty in his words, but it was no answer to her question. 'You think?'

He cocked his head. Fixed her with eyes that weren't distant or serene, but hot and compelling. 'I know.'

Heat whispered over Lise's cheeks. She found it difficult to accept his praise, especially when he was a master of palace games. The gentle compliments she'd fallen for once, losing herself completely to his words. Though Albert had said similar things about her, and she trusted what he'd said...

'I thought you'd be outside, mingling.' She waved her hand towards the open doorway. The murmur of voices and clink of cups on saucers floated into the room. 'With your adoring crowd. They like what you have to say.'

He had such command of everyone here. All the experts looked to him. Listened as he kept discussions on track, grabbed an odd idea before refashioning it into a brilliant solution. He was a true maverick. Watching his mind work was...

Thrilling.

When had she come to think of him this way, to rely on him? It seemed as natural as her next breath. He spread his arms wide and took a bow. 'They'll have enough pieces of me over the coming days. However I find the only person I wish to take from me, is you.'

It was impossible to catch her breath when he said things like that. The heat in her cheeks increased. 'I'm not sure that's a proper thing to say.'

'I'm not really one for being proper. But for now, there are other things on my mind.' He walked over towards a table in the corner, where a large pot of freshly brewed coffee stood. He poured some, added a lug of milk. One and a half sugars, exactly how she liked it. Rafe walked towards her holding out the cup. She accepted it and took a grateful sip. He'd asked how she took it only once. Every time since, each cup he'd made for her was perfect.

'You look...tired,' he said.

He wasn't wrong. The long, lonely nights worrying about how to fix the disaster left by her family seeped into her bones till they ached as if they were going to splinter.

'We're keeping the same hours. I'll be no more tired than you.'

Rafe scrubbed a hand over his unshaven jaw, the stubble a tantalising scratch under his fingertips. 'That may be, but I want to make sure you're looking after yourself. As your husband, I believe it's part of my job description.'

He stood closer now. The top button of his shirt undone, no tie. A smattering of dark hair hinted at the open neck of the pristine white shirt. On that strong chest, where he'd held her in the mountains, and she'd been lulled by his soothing heartbeat. What Lise wouldn't give to rest there again...

She shook her head. 'I need to fix this.' The choking frustration at the failure of her education threatened to throttle her.

He glanced outside at the milling group of people, then dropped his voice. 'And you will. The suggestion of reducing the size of the public service by natural attrition was all yours. You're taking on some of the austerity yourself. Selling the royal yacht.' It seemed an unnecessary extravagance, given that Lauritania was landlocked and the yacht had to be moored elsewhere. 'And Lance will be for ever in your debt for offering to sell antiques of value currently unused in the palace storerooms. Fiscal policy can be learned. But you have something that can't be. Humanity. A desire to build up the country's people, not take away.'

Lise drained the dregs of her coffee. Winced. 'I'm not unique in wanting those things for Lauritania.'

Rafe took the cup gently from her hands and placed it on the table.

'You care about inequality. Look at the organisations you supported.'

Her heart missed a few beats and Lise placed her hand to her chest, as if that would steady it. 'How do you know about them?'

She'd kept her involvement in some of the 'grittier' charities, as her father had called them, quiet. Seeking no accolades or plaudits for her work. She'd hoped if she kept her patronage private, her father would let her continue.

He hadn't.

'People who have a keen interest in our country were watching and appreciated what they saw.'

Her father had told her to leave any support to her brother, but Ferdinand hadn't been interested in funding shelters for young people or women escaping violence at home. That recollection tempered the flutter of surprise at the thought anyone paid much attention to what she did. The organisations she'd wanted to help most had suffered in her enforced absence. She dropped her head and twisted at her wedding band. 'Not everyone liked what they saw.'

'Your father was wrong for thinking you should stick to only saving stray puppies and kittens.' Lise stopped toying with the ring on her finger and looked up at him. Rafe and the King must have spoken of this, all those times they'd discussed her future without her. She tried to muster some semblance of anger or indignance but the flame of it guttered out and died in the warmth of Rafe's approval.

'They're worthy causes,' she said. Though she'd never been allowed to own a rescue kitten or a puppy, for all the public support she'd given them. Only pedigreed animals were allowed in the palace.

'They are.' Rafe nodded. 'But you wanted to do more. People noticed. Like when you were forced to give up competitive skiing. Everyone heard what your father had to say, that you were concentrating on your formal duties since you'd come of age. What people saw was your quiet acceptance of the role being formed for you.'

Not the role she wanted. Never that. What she'd wanted didn't matter.

'Maybe the tantrums happened behind closed doors,' she said. Though they hadn't. Not then. Her moment had been reserved for a day when the illusion of a hopeful future with a man she might love had been crushed under the King's handmade shoe.

'Perhaps. But you were headed for a world championship to represent your country. Tantrums would have been forgiven, in that instance.'

She shook her head. A strand of hair fell from her chignon. Rafe reached out, hesitated a moment—a pause between breaths—then slipped the unruly piece behind her ear. A shimmer of pleasure skittered down her spine.

'I know the people found it unfair you couldn't finish what you started,' Rafe said.

'What people?'

She'd only ever heard what her family had to say about her failings, not about her successes.

'Your loyal, obedient subjects, of which I am one.'

'Oh, no, now you're being too much.' She snorted. 'You've never had an obedient day in your life.'

Rafe moved close and she could smell the citrus of his aftershave and the cool undertone like the autumn breeze in the mountains that she would associate with him for ever. Then he leaned down and murmured into her ear, 'I can choose to be if I wish. Most people aren't worthy.'

'And I am?'

'There are people who saw you as an integral part of Lauritania's future, not a footnote to it.'

'You have such faith in me.' The crown they'd placed on her head at her coronation had been too heavy. As if it didn't fit. As if the role of Queen wasn't meant for her at all. Now, with Rafe's support, she was beginning to believe it was.

Beginning to believe that this role might be one she could turn into her own…

'You have a passion and drive Hasselbeck and his cronies don't understand. They want everything to stay the same, which requires a compliant monarch. You'll never be that, and she's your reminder,' he said, nodding to the painting of her great-great-grandmother on the wall. People began drifting back into the room and taking their place at the grand table that dominated it. Rafe took no notice of them, his only attention to her, as if not another person in this place mattered.

'They're afraid you'll believe in yourself. And when you do, they fear the Queen you'll become.'

CHAPTER TEN

RAFE WOKE IN the darkness and checked his phone. Three in the morning. He turned. Under the door to Lise's room cut a sliver of light. Strange that she'd be awake this early. He rolled out of bed, went to the walk-in wardrobe, and threw on a pair of pyjama bottoms, no shirt. He knew Lise enjoyed seeing him half dressed. Any tantalising lick of her gaze over his bare skin gave him hope that soon this cold war between them would end. And he needed it to end. Being close to her and not touching. Not kissing. No silken skin sliding over his as they immersed themselves in the heady pleasure of each other's bodies. It had begun to consume him, till Lise was all he could think about. His silent obsession. The meagre taste he'd had would never be enough for the addict he'd become.

He walked to the door between their rooms and knocked without an answer. Knocked again, louder this time. No sound came from the room beyond, so he opened the door and went through.

A lamp glowed in the corner. The bed turned down but not slept in, the sheets pristine. He checked the expansive en-suite bathroom, but nothing. She hadn't slept here. Lise had been tired over dinner. Pale skin, dusty shadows under her red-tinged eyes. Yawning when she'd thought he'd not been looking. She'd drunk coffee. Espresso. Strong. Not her usual preference. Looked worn and frayed at the edges after days of trying to bring Lauritania back from the brink.

They would succeed. Failure was not an option. So he tried to stitch her together as much as he could, when it appeared as if she might unravel. But she hadn't yet. Lise had been underestimated by her family, her government and, in the past, by herself. Now she was working harder than anyone to keep it together and no one could doubt she was growing into a force to be reckoned with.

He walked back to his room and dragged on a shirt before padding barefoot down the chilly halls of a disappearing autumn, in search of her.

Rafe wanted to spend the cold, snow-covered season in bed with Lise, keeping each other warm in the best of ways. On bleak days of wind and sleet they could take time being wrapped in each other. A fantasy, perhaps, but he believed they'd made inroads. She seemed freer, happier. Like the hopeful Princess she'd once been. It was a pleasure to witness.

As he moved through the palace everything lay dark and quiet. Paintings of Lise's ancestors glaring down at him as he looked for her. He didn't care. To hell with all of them. They hadn't cared for Lise. Her father, mother, brother. Leaving her to fix the mess they'd neglected without any preparation. He strode to the pool where she might have gone for a swim, as he knew she sometimes did from the night staff who kept a hidden watch for her safety from darkened alcoves. Sadly, the pavilion sat empty. Moonlight shimmering on the water through the glass above. He travelled back past their suites towards the study, which was the only other place he thought she might have gone if she'd remained in the palace.

As Rafe reached the room a streak of light shone from underneath the dark oak. The door lay open a crack, so he pushed his way in. Lise slumped over her desk, head on her arms. Asleep. The computer screen on, a royal crest sliding lazily across the lock screen. An empty teacup and pot sat abandoned in a corner. The fresh herbal smell made him smile a little, that she drank his own family's concoction.

On the desktop were scattered papers covered in her elegant, looped script. Notes. Scratchings. Ideas. He didn't look too closely though, transfixed by her face. Her pale lashes feathered on even paler cheeks.

'Ahh, Lise.' She was dressed for the bed she'd not slept in. A robe wrapped round her, grey and soft. He reached out, stroked her hair. Brushed a few silky strands from her forehead. She didn't stir, other than a long, slow breath in and out.

It couldn't be comfortable lying there, which told him how exhausted she was. She needed to sleep late. As it was the weekend now, Lise could. They didn't have anything that couldn't be moved. A meeting approving the final arrangements for the Queen's Ball was all that stood in her way in the early morning. He wanted her to sleep late with him, but she'd unlikely accept that yet, as much as he wanted to tuck her into his body and keep her safe. Instead, he'd settle for taking her to her room. Rafe moved in close, manoeuvred one arm round her curved back, another under her legs and scooped her slender frame high into his arms. She stirred then. Protested in a sleepy kind of way as her body stiffened into consciousness. He held her close. Stilled for a moment as she squirmed.

'Shh…' he murmured. 'You fell asleep at your desk, love. Lay your head down.' He waited a heartbeat. Two. Absorbed the sleepy mumble of something that made no sense. He waited another second as Lise draped an arm over his shoulder, snuggled her head into his neck, and he relished the feel of her in his arms again.

In sleep, Lise's body told the truth of her and him. He moved silently towards her room, accepting a moment in time with her in his arms. Carried her inside where the temptation to curl up with her almost overwhelmed him. Reaching her bed, he bent over to lay her on the covers.

As he did, Lise gripped him tight, and clung to him with a whimper of distress. *'No.'*

He straightened and she nuzzled into him, her breath ghosting across his neck. Rafe stood for a few moments, letting her settle back into sleep. She grew heavy in his arms again. He rested his head against hers, breathing in the scent of wildflowers, which he'd come to think of now as her own. She needed to sleep long and soundly, yet she didn't want him to let her go. The solution was obvious.

He manoeuvred into the bed with her still in his arms. She opened her eyes then. Confused, still mostly asleep the way they looked at him dreamy and unfocussed. Rafe lay back, taking her with him.

'Rest now,' he said as he stroked his hand over Lise's side. Absorbing her long, contented exhale as her head nestled into his shoulder, her hand over his heart.

He reached out and turned off the bedside light. A lassitude stole over him. Borne by tiredness, sure. He and Lise had both been working long and hard. Still, it was more. Something strange and foreign that he took a while to recognise. A bone-deep contentment that he was finally where he should be again. She might hate him in the morning; he would deal with her disapprobation then. But having her in his arms again? That was worth it.

Lise's heart pounded as she grappled to find purchase on something, anything. She had to hold on. She couldn't let go, yet she couldn't recall why. But she was falling.

Falling.

She gasped, trying to suck in the air that never seemed enough. Trying to breathe but the breaths wouldn't come. Clutching onto the first thing she could reach.

'Lise. Shh… I have you.'

The rough caress of a voice. Where was she? Lise opened her eyes. Blinked at the soft light of a new day. In her bed, on her side, with her hands clenching around clumps of a man's T-shirt.

'You had a bad dream.' Rafe. She couldn't release his shirt, her hands clamped in place over the scrunched fabric. Bad things happened if she let people go. 'I found you asleep at your desk and tried to put you to bed. You held onto me.'

She remembered now. Numbers. Too many numbers that screeched at her in urgency and hurt her eyes as she tried to sort through finances that made little sense. She'd put her head down on her desk for only a few moments. To rest. Then she'd woken cradled safe like a child in strong arms. Weightless, being carried. Till that sensation of being let go and she grabbed on tight.

The shivering started, a quake through her body. 'I'm cold. Rafe, why am I always so cold?'

He wrapped his arms round her, drawing her close to the hard heat of him. 'I don't know, but I'm here.' He dropped his forehead to hers. Holding her till the shivering subsided and she was lax and soft in his embrace. She lay there, his body warmth sliding over her. Aware now of their legs and feet entwined. The bulk of his muscles and jut of strong bones. Soaking in the pleasure of it all as he held her tighter to his body. The care he'd taken, demanding nothing for himself. Every part of him raw and male and uncompromising as she lay flush against him. Especially…

Oh.

He shifted and the hard length of him pressed into her stomach.

Yes.

She pulled back to look at him. His dark curls unruly across his forehead. The shadow of stubble peppering his jaw. Lise smoothed her hands over his chest, where his shirt sat crushed by her fingers. Mapping the defined landscape of his body. His eyes scanned her face, dropped to her lips. She reached out and traced his jaw, the roughness teasing her fingertips. They reached his mouth and he nipped at them. Heat rushed through her, the desire overwhelming, here in his arms. The scent of him all fresh and crisp and wild like the cold air of his craggy mountain home. It made her crave to simply give into the relentless need throbbing through her with every heartbeat. To claim a wildness, a freedom for herself once more. She canted her hips into him, and he pinned her with an incendiary gaze.

'Be sure,' he growled, feral and raw. The sensual warning rippled through her, an exquisite ache blooming deep inside. As their bodies rubbed together, he tipped his head back, closed his eyes and moaned, the salacious sound setting her ablaze. She pressed her lips to the strong column of his exposed throat. Breathed in the musky scent of his skin.

The only time she felt warm was with him. The only time the crippling guilt had been silenced was in his arms, her fears annihilated by his lips and hands. There was something about him that made her want to laugh again. Made her feel strong and capable, like the Queen she'd been crowned rather than the lost Princess who'd first taken the throne. None of this had been easy, trying to save the country, but this glorious man, he had faith in her, believed in her. And she'd begun to believe in herself too, that maybe she didn't have to burn everything to the ground, but simply change what didn't work and keep the rest. And why, in the process, shouldn't she take something for herself? Stop fighting and give into pleasure for once?

'I'm sure.'

His gaze was intent, hot. Boring into her as if he could see her soul. 'Do we need protection? I have none in this room.'

He'd thought of that, her refusal to fall pregnant, when she would have forgotten everything for him in this moment. A rush of heat flooded her, like being immersed in hot water. She gripped his shirt hard. Shook her head. Her cycle was regular and her period due any day.

'No. It's a safe time.'

'My health checks are clear.'

'I trust you,' she whispered, realising the blinding truth of her words in this moment. She hadn't thought she'd trust anyone again, but somehow Rafe had slid his way through her defences.

Then her world flipped, and she lay underneath Rafe. Pressed deep into the mattress. His hips cradled between her thighs. The hardness of him *there, right there*. Her hands moved under his shirt, running over the tense muscles of his back. She slid them down his spine, relishing the quiver of flesh under her palm. The whole of her burning up in the bed.

He kissed her neck and she trembled, his teeth scraping the sensitive flesh at the junction of her shoulder. She slipped her hands beneath the waistband of his pyjamas to his backside, the muscles flexing and releasing as he rocked against her. Both fully clothed yet it was as if they had nothing on. The curl of pleasure tightening inside. His fingers circled her nipple through the soft fabric she wore. She writhed underneath him, trying to get closer as he dropped his head and sucked before pulling away. She whimpered in protest.

'You need something, Lise?'

The feel of him, hard and strong as she ground into him. 'Too many clothes.'

She tugged his shirt over his head, and he tossed it on the floor. Mouth on hers, teeth clashing as he plundered her. No finesse, no softness but a taking. She gave back, her tongue curling with his, their panting breaths filling the room. He raked her thin robe from her shoulders then lifted her top. Lise shrugged both off, she and Rafe tangled in each other as they wrestled out of the remaining clothing until they were deliciously naked. Hands roaming and searching. Goosebumps peppered her body.

'Getting cold again? I'll keep you warm.' Rafe stroked his hands lower, teasing her inner thighs. 'Open for me.'

His voice a rough demand that sent another

shiver through her. She relaxed her legs, breaths coming in short gusts. Squirming against his clever fingers, teasing her close to where she needed, but not close enough. The sensation in her body empty, unquenched. Rafe traced his lips along the shell of her ear, murmuring about her perfection, how responsive she was for him as the maddening stroke on her inner thighs continued. Then one hand left its ministrations. She groaned. The sound was greeted with a wicked chuckle, which rumbled through her.

'Patience,' he murmured, the breath tickling at her ear, 'will be rewarded.'

The fingertips of his right hand brushed her nipple. She arched her back, catlike, craving more contact than these frustrating teases. Her reward was his thumb and forefinger, rolling the too sensitive flesh between them.

She writhed. Desperate. Wanting him to fill the emptiness inside her. He didn't move. Other than to keep up the torture of her nipple, each touch sending electric shocks between her legs. His free hand continuing to stroke her inner thigh, driving her mad.

She shifted against him to try and get his hands closer. Moaning unintelligible things. 'Please, please, Rafe.'

'I love it when you beg for pleasure,' he said, voice harsh and strained. The weight of his own desire, bold and heavy against her leg as he tormented her. That frustrating hand of his dipping low to slide between her legs. He stroked, gently at first. Driving her higher and higher. She wasn't cold now. Her body a furnace. All she needed was relief. She chased it with mindless determination.

He rose above her, the blunt head of him between her legs. Slowly, so slowly, easing inside as he held her gaze.

'Whatever you need,' he whispered. 'I don't want to hurt you.'

Rafe's voice rippled through her as he gave her what she craved. She burned for him as he slid deep into her body. Her spine arching at the exquisite pressure, the fullness.

'You aren't. Please. Please, Rafe.'

He stopped and stared, looking deep into her eyes. The muscles of his neck straining as he held himself still above her, but there was something else. Something passing across his face. Myriad emotions that washed over him then were gone, heated things that spoke of desire and possession and something else that made her breath catch.

'Tilt up,' he murmured, stroking a hand down her body, under the swell of her backside. 'Wrap your legs round mine. Move with me.'

She did, joining him in the rhythm of their lovemaking, as he filled her over and over till the fire ignited inside her. Building to something exquisite, irrevocable. She moved with Rafe as she let it take her, hurtling her towards the edge.

'Come for me, Lise, for *me*.'

In this moment, she didn't care about duty or responsibility. Only the feel of him against her. Rough against smooth. Hard against soft.

'*Rafe!*' She shouted his name without shame. Gripping him as the waves of pleasure crashed over her. Her cries reverberating through the room as Rafe captured her mouth in a deep, unrelenting kiss.

Rafe circled the edge of the maelstrom as Lise fell, his body taut and primed only for her. Nothing prepared him for the beauty of her in ecstasy. The glorious flush of pink painted her skin. Her body rigid and panting, possessed by the pleasure of their joining. His mind blanked of anything bar the silken grasp of her body. He kissed her trembling lips, her breaths hard and fast as he thrust into the dark, wet heat at the centre of her.

Finally Lise was his.

Her hands tangled in his hair, the pleasure excruciating. They moved in a dance he knew too well but was nothing like he'd experienced before. Surging forwards, not so gentle now. This all-consuming desire to win, possess, pleasure.

Something more than sex, a craving that only she could sate.

The noises she made, soft, mewling sounds. The gasps, the slide of bodies. Her softness under his palms. His own moans as the grip of her drove him wild. The prickle at the base of his spine, the heaviness that told him he was close, so close.

He ran a thumb over her nipple. Took it between his fingers and rolled as she moaned loud and long. A flutter deep inside her and he knew she was close again. He craved her pleasure once more. Pushed her harder, faster. She met him stroke for stroke.

Her body stiffened and grabbed him tight as she arched back. There was no holding on, the edge rushed up and he hurled himself over into the storm that was his wife.

As everything fell back into place around them, she softened into him. Relaxed as he stroked his hands over her silken skin, as the tremors subsided.

'We'll spend the day in bed,' he murmured. His voice unfamiliar to his own ears. Rough and full of lust. A promise of things to come.

'The whole palace will have heard us.' Lise whispered the words. He wasn't sure why, when only moments before she'd screamed his name.

And he craved it. The acknowledgement that

they were together now, not just on paper, but in truth. Rafe traced his lips over the shell of her ear. A growl, full of heat and possession so she could never forget this moment.

'Let the whole palace know you're mine.'

CHAPTER ELEVEN

THE COLOUR AND light of the palace's grandest ballroom swirled around her. People in their finest dresses and most opulent jewels glittered under the glow of pendulous chandeliers. The monarch's annual ball was one of the most anticipated events on Lauritania's social calendar. Lise looked around at the decorations, flowers. The food and wine. All she saw was the rivers of money lost on frivolous things when the country's finances were on a knife edge. Still, the country looked forward to the ball as if it heralded a new beginning. This year, the date signifying the Queen and her people out of official mourning.

Lise took a moment to herself, sipping at her glass of champagne, the bubbles tingling in her mouth. *'Little bubbles of happiness'* her mother had called them when Lise was introduced to the drink for the first time on her sixteenth birthday. Still, she wasn't convinced joy was found in the sparkle of this fine vintage. What did soften the sharp edges was Rafe. She peered over the top of her glass at her husband. Strange how that word now fitted as comfortably as old clothes. Though nothing about him could be described as old, or comfortable. Certainly not the dinner suit exquisitely crafted to mould every hard line of his body. A body that seemed perfectly honed to pleasure hers. Like this afternoon, when she should have been preparing for the ball. Instead, trying on her trousseau, which hadn't quite made it to the palace collection, despite her initial intentions. She'd wanted to surprise him tonight. Instead, he'd found her in her room. Slipped the cobweb-fine silk and embroidered confection wordlessly over her skin, laid her out on the bed. A flood of heat coursed through her. He'd been insatiable as he'd kissed down her body and she'd threaded her hands through his unruly curls. Her cries ringing through the bedroom as he'd feasted...

'Your Majesty.'

Lise turned. Put on her formal smile. Ignoring the sliver of disappointment that she couldn't immerse herself in the memories of the indulgent afternoon any longer. But the night was drawing to a close. Soon she could be in Rafe's arms again.

'Prime Minister.'

Whilst it probably wasn't the done thing to think about Rafe making love to her whilst talking to Hasselbeck, her body wasn't so keen to keep her libido in the box she attempted to push it back into. Every part of her flushed, hot and needy. All for Rafe. Always for him. His power to make her scream was only matched by his ability to make her laugh again. He'd firmly entrenched himself as her obsession. Her counsel, her rock of support.

'Your announcement regarding Lauritania's financial woes seems to have been a success.'

Hasselbeck's words weren't meant as a commendation. She dragged herself back into the conversation when he was the last person she wanted to speak to. He'd never rated her, and it was something she wouldn't easily forget.

'People will understand the difficult decisions if everyone shares in them. Those who have the most should proportionally bear the greatest burden.'

The prime minister's face pinched, as if he'd sucked a lemon. He wanted her to fail. She knew it. She glanced at Rafe once more, now holding court with the British ambassador. In complete command of everyone and everything around him. He looked up, their eyes met, and he winked. Another rush of heat licked over her, no doubt pinking her skin. One more black mark on her queenly abilities because queens probably shouldn't blush. Though Lise wasn't sure she really cared any more about what she should and shouldn't do in her role as monarch. She was turning it into her own in ways she'd not thought possible, and Lauritanians seemed to be happy with their new King and Queen…

The prime minister followed her gaze in Rafe's direction. 'It seems marriage to His Majesty suits you.'

The media had been fed carefully crafted stories about their relationship. The breathless reporting of a happy union buoying the people. To Lise, that reporting now felt real. She touched her neck where a scrape from Rafe's stubble lay hidden under concealer. The make-up artist smirking as she'd obliterated the evidence of the afternoon's lovemaking. She loved Rafe's marks of possession on her skin. Owning every part of her. She trembled at the ripple of recollected pleasure.

'It does.'

Hasselbeck leaned in, almost conspiratorially. Lise tried not to shrink away. People were now watching them, and she didn't need any talk of instability or a rift between her and her prime minister, not when her whole country's future was at stake. She pasted a fake smile on her face and gulped some champagne.

'You know he went to school with my son? The De Villiers family always had grand aspirations. His Majesty was the most ambitious, even then.'

She forced out a laugh, when she really wanted to hiss that Rafe was worth a thousand times more than anyone else in the room. They paled when compared to him.

'There's nothing wrong with aspiring to be better. It's a noble endeavour,' she said as Hassel-beck's attention flicked over her shoulder. At the same time, the back of her neck tingled with a familiar warmth.

'Talking about me?'

Rafe's voice was cool and distant. Full of disdain. She looked at him, stiff and formal. Gone was the relaxed, smiling man who'd been charming dignitaries only minutes earlier.

'We were just saying what a supportive consort you are for the Queen. It's pleasant to see some happiness in the palace.' Hasselbeck smiled, showing too many teeth. 'Indeed, Lady Conrad appears to be finding fresh happiness too if rumour is correct. With the best man from your wedding… His Majesty's friend.'

Lise reeled. Sara, with… Lance? She had no doubt he was a charmer, that much had been evident from her meeting with him in the castle. But he was a player too, by Rafe's account. She couldn't imagine Sara in the slightest bit interested in someone like that.

Though an expression flickered across Rafe's face that seemed…knowing. He placed his hand on the small of her back, flexed his fingers.

'Yes,' Rafe said. 'She had a desire to see England and His Grace offered her a seat on his private jet.'

Lise's champagne flute almost slipped from her

grasp. How did Rafe know when she didn't? She downed the last of her drink then placed the glass on the tray of a server walking past.

'How convenient for Lady Sara,' Hasselbeck said with a sneer.

'Most,' Rafe replied. 'I'm sure you'd agree everyone deserves occasional respite from the demands of duty or family expectation. Now, the hour is late. It's time Her Majesty and I retired.'

Lise tried not to show any emotion as Rafe guided her towards the exit, her stomach clenching in the twin emotions of shock and hurt. Their formal departure was announced. She smiled at the crowd from muscle memory alone. Rafe had agreed to no more secrets between them. Yet she'd been trying to get in touch with Sara since the wedding and had heard *nothing*. What was going on? She felt bloodless. Frozen. As if every part of her were hewn from ice. As they left the ballroom Rafe removed his hand from her lower back and the freeze intensified.

'What the hell was that?' she spat.

'Not here.' Rafe quelled her with a frigid glance then smiled at a member of staff, who bowed as they passed.

She tried to muster the disdain that had come so naturally to the rest of her family. If he wanted indifferent, she could do that. Lise allowed the chill to seep through her veins again, obliterating all the warmth Rafe had brought to her life.

She'd asked for truths and had been fed a lie by omission. What else had been going on when she hadn't been paying attention? She'd find out or be damned trying. As Lise walked to their rooms, she wondered whether she could believe anything Rafe said, ever again.

Rafe strode through the palace halls to their suite, jaw clenched. As they reached the entrance it was all he could do not to fling back the door and stalk inside. Instead, he allowed Lise to sweep past him in her dress of ethereal grey, dotted with crystals that glittered with every move. She'd asked, *'What the hell?'* Yet after overhearing her conversation with the prime minister, he could well ask the same.

Aspiring to be better?

What had she meant by that?

Lise moved to the window staring out at the view, her gown and jewels sparkling in the lamplight. Her mother had been renowned as an icy beauty, remote and untouchable. Right now, Lise was her mother incarnate.

This was not how the evening was meant to end, in some pointless cold war. Cold was not what he looked for when it came to Lise. He tugged at his bow tie. Shrugged off his jacket and tossed it onto a chair. Undid the tight top button of his shirt so that it didn't throttle him. How she'd dazzled the ballroom, finally out of mourning black. Tonight, all eyes had been on the young Queen and all he could think was that this magnificent woman was *his*, in every way.

Yet she seemed to believe he was on some *noble endeavour* to *improve* himself. As if he wasn't good enough. Rafe clenched his fists, relaxed them, and flexed his fingers. There would be an explanation, there must be. He and Lise hadn't been apart since their first time of making love. Each night spent in bed together, a passion and hunger for each other that wouldn't be denied. Each day working to save the country. They were building something, as he'd known they would. Something solid and untouchable. Hasselbeck and his cronies could keep their grubby intrigues away from it.

He tried shaking away the dark simmer of anger that bubbled in his gut. She turned to him, the diamonds fire against her throat. A stark contrast to her glacial gaze. He took a steadying breath, not trusting himself to say anything in this moment. Instead, he removed his cufflinks and placed them on a bureau, began rolling up his shirtsleeves.

'When were you going to tell me about Sara?' Lise's voice was low and cool like the autumn chill whistling under the eaves. It was a surprise that she appeared unaware Sara had left Lauritania. Necessitating him making his own disclosures to hide Lise's shock and stop the prime minister fishing for trouble between them.

'There's nothing to tell. She wanted to leave the country and needed a passport. I signed her application. She went.'

'You signed her passport application? She's *my* friend. My brother's fiancée...' Something about Lise's face crumpled, before she stiffened her spine and smoothed out her expression into frigid disdain. 'And you decided I didn't need to know?'

He shrugged.

'You were grieving.' And surely if Sara wanted Lise to find out she would have said something herself. 'And I thought—'

'I *demanded* no secrets from you.' Lise clenched her fists, the whole of her tight and shaking. 'Yet you kept this from me. I had to find out from Hasselbeck, a man who's determined to humiliate me. How could you?'

'How could *I*?' This conversation was skidding off track in ways difficult to control. Rafe held up his hands, trying to placate her. To stop her vibrating with barely controlled fury. All the while his blood surged with the furious adrenaline of his own growing outrage. 'You seemed to be fine friends, laughing at my attempts at...*self-improvement*.'

She stalked towards him.

'I could hardly entertain a pitched battle with my prime minister on the floor of the palace ballroom,' she hissed. 'But let me ask you this, since your ambition is renowned. Would you have married me if I were simply Lise Betencourt? Would you have loved me if I were a mere commoner? Not the Princess or the Queen?'

It was as if he'd been doused in iced water. Love? When had that word entered their discussion?

'We have passion and purpose.' More than either of them could have hoped for at the beginning of their marriage. Love? That was meaningless. He moved towards her, slow and steady. Trying to suppress the urge to shout. To make her see. 'But we are who we are and can't change that fact. So your question's meaningless.'

She threw up her hands. 'It means *everything*. You wanted the Crown. The country. The power. Never me. *Never* me.'

Lise curled into herself then. It looked as if she were being sawn in two. 'But that's fine because you became King and one of the most powerful men in Europe.' Her voice faded. Quiet and defeated. He hated that tone. Better she rage and scream at him rather than this, devoid of emotion as it was.

Rafe stepped forwards, closer now. Close

enough to see the sparkle of welling tears before she blinked them furiously away. 'Lise—'

'Don't use my name.'

'Why?'

She jabbed her finger at him. 'I am not and have never been Lise to you. All you ever saw was Her Most Serene and Ethereal Majesty. Defender of the Realm. Annalise Marie Betencourt. Queen of Lauritania. And that's exactly whom you shall have, from this moment onwards.'

His jaw tightened. He breathed through a furnace of heat raging in his gut. He would get through to her in the end. 'You're chasing shadows, things that aren't real, whereas this, how we work together, *that's* something honest and truthful.'

'You want to talk about truth now?' She raised her chin and glared at him. 'I see you for who you are. The ambitious farm boy who coveted the Crown and acquired it.'

Rafe jerked back. And there it was. He couldn't have taken a more direct hit if she'd slapped him. He'd always believed Lise was different from the rest. That in him she saw something more than his history, his past. Yet in the end what they might have shared was meaningless. The words he'd overheard tonight with Hasselbeck were *her* truth. Lise was still Lauritania's aristocracy, and he was the common dirt upon which she trod.

'You go too far,' he snapped. The pulse roared in his ears. 'Ask yourself one thing whilst you sit there on your lofty throne. Where would you or the country be without me? You'd be nothing more than a mouthpiece for the prime minister.'

Lise narrowed her eyes, hard, cold and unreachable. 'Better than a puppet of yours.'

He shook his head. How could he have been fooled? No matter the alluring wrapping, they were all the same, these blue bloods. Only one of their own was good enough. He'd always be the outsider.

'If that's what you believe there's nothing more to say.' He bowed deep and low, like the commoner he was. 'Good evening, Your Majesty.'

Rafe snatched his great-grandfather's cufflinks from the bureau and stormed from the room, slamming the door shut behind him. He'd never be enough for the government, for the people, for her. Lise wanted to be Queen on her own? She could do it and to hell with how heavy the crown sat on her head. He grabbed the solid iron key from the side table, shoved it in the keyhole of the great oak door between them and twisted.

The lock tumbled closed with an emphatic, satisfying click.

CHAPTER TWELVE

LISE STARED OUT of the window of her study. Autumn now firmly taking hold of the countryside, the trees turning gold. Soon the frost would start, the creep and clutch of winter gripping the mountains. But it was always winter for her. Especially now.

She hadn't seen Rafe for two days. He hadn't come to any meals. No light shone out from under the door of his adjoining room at night. The *locked* door. The ache of it twisted hard in her stomach. The hurt still as sharp as the night of the ball. His lack of honesty when he'd promised no more secrets. When she'd realised that yet another person couldn't love her. But there was more. Her memories of his widened eyes, the visceral pain on his face as he'd reared back at her words.

'The ambitious farm boy who coveted the Crown...'

She loathed being cruel and wasn't proud of what she'd said because she knew what those words would do to him. She'd asked him once did he believe she'd hurt him and now she knew the answer in his silence that day was *yes*. For she *had* hurt him in the end. Coldly, deliberately. As he'd hurt her too, although that didn't excuse her own actions. He'd never wanted Lise Betencourt. He'd wanted the Crown, the Queen. Status, nothing more.

She realised now the trap she'd laid for herself. Somewhere deep inside she'd hoped that he could love her, as she'd fallen in love with him. Because that was why she was standing here, with her heart aching as if it had taken a mortal blow. She was in love. Try as she might to fool her head otherwise, she couldn't. Love had caught her when she'd least expected it. When it wasn't hers to wish for.

But why? She wasn't sure any more. She'd spent so many years believing no one could love her, it seemed to have become self-fulfilling. Yet she understood now that, before loving another, she needed to learn to love herself. Lise pulled her jacket tighter, hugging it to her body. Whilst she didn't like herself for what she'd said to Rafe, she'd come to realise one thing. She was *worthy*. Of the many things Rafe might have said to her, on one, he'd been correct. She'd survived, become stronger as a person. Grown as Queen. It was a role she didn't disdain any longer because a person sitting on the throne could do great things, great good. That was something Rafe had taught her. A painful lesson, but she finally recognised her worth as a woman. Didn't she deserve to live a life full of joy and love, for herself?

Her marriage was hollow, sure. Fantasies that it was something more scoured clean away. So, what was left? She couldn't divorce. The stability of the country and the fragile steps to repairing the economy relied on Rafe and her together. *Jusqu'à la mort. Until death.* Rafe had warned her all along with those words engraved on the inner side of her wedding ring. A ring that sat like the weight of the planet on her finger.

She lifted her hand to look at the exquisite gold and enamel band. As she did, a part of the intricate design snagged on the wool of her skirt, and something pulled free. A golden panel like a tiny door, upon which one of the delicate, enamelled flowers lay embellished. Lise peered at it, because there was something engraved underneath the panel, on the body of the ring.

Mon coeur. My heart.

Pulse racing, she tore the ring from her finger. She'd thought the panels were merely a part of the intricate design, not hiding any message. She flicked open another with her fingernail.

Mon ame. My soul.

Then another, and another.

Mon debut. Ma fin. My beginning. My end.

She twisted the ring between her thumb and forefinger. The whole message laid out for her to

see. The secret she'd worn every day since Rafe
had slipped it on her finger.

My heart, my soul. My beginning, my end.
Until death.

Her eyes blurred with the sting of tears, which
slid onto her cheeks. Those words. How she'd always dreamed of a man thinking of her this way.
The kind of soaring passion she craved. But what
of it? The ring was a family heirloom, that much
she knew. Still, why give her something so deeply
sentimental if it meant nothing?

She pressed her hand to her aching heart. Unable to move or breathe. Could the message on
the ring be…a start? What if…? She didn't know,
her thoughts a tangle once more. She looked at
the ring again. Being in love made you vulnerable, meant that you could be hurt. What if, like
her fear of being unloved, Rafe feared that loving
her would mean he'd be hurt again?

Which was exactly what she had done.

She heard it then. A gentle knock. A respectful
cough. Lise wheeled around, brushing away the
tears that marred her cheeks. *Albert.* For a moment, she allowed the sting of disappointment at
seeing her private secretary, rather than her husband.

He entered the room, face full of sympathy. 'I
have some news about Lady Conrad.'

'Yes?' She'd asked Albert to find out what had

gone on, since Sara hadn't responded to her attempts. What was another rejection to add to the ever-growing list? Lise dreaded what he might say but needed to hear it all the same.

'The English tabloids report a whirlwind romance and engagement. I haven't been able to speak with her myself. I'm sure she'll be in touch when she can. She's likely afraid you'll be hurt, so soon…after.'

Relief mingled with confusion and dismay. Rafe had said something similar.

You were grieving…

Something cracked inside that she was not sure would ever come together again. Even though their betrothal had been arranged, Lise had always trusted that Ferdinand and her best friend loved each other in some way. What else was she kidding herself to believe, which had no basis in truth? She took a slow breath to steady herself.

'Thank you, Albert.'

He nodded to the ring, still gripped in her now quaking fingers.

'I'd heard a rumour of its wonders, but thought it impolite to ask,' he said in almost reverent tones, holding out his hand. 'May I?'

Lise hesitated. She didn't want to relinquish it, still not having come to grips with the words' meaning, if anything at all. But Albert was like a father to her, so she dropped the ring into his palm. He turned it round, inspecting the enamel flowers. Reading the messages. A soft smile playing on his face.

'The Crown jeweller was asked to ensure it was sound prior to the wedding. That it was fit for a Queen.' He looked up at her, tears once more flowing freely down her cheeks, and a tiny frown creased his brow. 'Is there anything else I might do for you, Lise?'

He was allowing her to be the woman, not his monarch.

'I made a mistake, marrying him.' Her voice cracked. Thinking it was one thing, admitting it to someone like Albert... 'Rafe wanted to be King. He didn't want me.'

'How could he *not* want you?'

That was the crucial question. 'I—I don't know.'

Albert looked at the ring, snapped the little enamel doors firmly shut, hiding its secrets once more, then he handed it back to her. The golden band sat warm and heavy in her palm. 'A man who gives a woman this—'

She shook her head. 'It was apparently his great-grandmother's.'

'He could have had a new ring made. One with no messages at all, yet this was the wedding ring he chose.' Albert reached out and closed her fingers around the ring, engulfing her hand in his.

'You need to believe you're deserving of what it says.'

She was trying to, but there was so much still to repair it seemed insurmountable. 'I wasn't... kind to him.'

'People who are afraid often aren't.' He let her go, clasping his hands behind his back. 'Do you know why I stayed on as your private secretary when I could have retired?'

She shrugged. 'I assumed you loved the role.'

He sighed. Shook his head. 'I saw how your family held you to a different standard. That was unfair. I am immeasurably proud of the girl you were and the woman you've become. So I stayed for you. Lise, you might now be my Queen, but you've *always* been like the daughter I never had. I remain because I love *you* and I'm here for as long as you need me.'

'Albert.' More tears flooded her eyes. When would they ever stop? She walked towards him, engulfed him in a hug. He returned it in a heart-felt embrace.

When they pulled apart, he withdrew a hand-kerchief from his pocket and handed it to her. She gave a tremulous laugh, patting at her eyes.

'Oh, dear, you're going to be with me for ever.'

'It will be my greatest privilege. Now go and claim what you want. What you deserve.' His smile was gentle and kind as he bowed and took his leave.

She placed the ring on her finger once more, its weight now a comfort rather than a curse. She loved Rafe. She *deserved* that love. He'd once said she could rewrite the fairy tale and she would. Their time began now.

She would fight for Rafe to love her.

Rafe lay on the bed staring at the limewashed ceiling. He hadn't run here. He didn't run from anything. It was more to regroup. Coming to his mountain home, to contemplate the habits of a lifetime. Two days were all he'd allowed himself. To hike the high pastures and remind himself of who he was, because he'd lost his way, and a chance with Lise in the process.

Shame sat heavily on him, a weight almost too much to bear. Lise had been right. He'd wanted the power. But the power of a king didn't change who he was. A farm boy. And he *had* been ashamed of his heritage, he recognised. If he hadn't he would never have been driven to the position he was in now. Forgetting the truth of himself. The things he'd learned from his parents in these mountains, about hard work and never shirking your duty, reminding him of the kind of man he was meant to be.

The ambitious farm boy who coveted the

Crown. Yes, he was all those things, and the crown that he'd so craved was a hollow one. He wasn't proud of how he'd got here. Lise had once thought she was the fraud. Yet she was the one who'd tried living true to herself, in the end taking up a role she'd never wanted because of her duty to her country. The only fraud was him. The crown on his head hadn't made him better than anyone. They still saw what they wanted to see. The pretender. When this…the old house, the history of his family, was enough. It always had been.

He'd kept a secret from her, a small one perhaps, but she'd demanded complete honesty and he hadn't given it to her, only feeding her insecurities. Leading to an argument that played into both of their fears. His regret in that regard was deep and complete…

The shrill ring of his phone had him leaping from the bed to a side table where it lay vibrating. He checked the screen, but the number wasn't Lise's. It was the prime minister. He gritted his teeth. The man would pay for hurting Lise. His days in his job were numbered. Rafe swiped to answer.

'What do you want, Hasselbeck?'

'Her Majesty.' Hasselbeck's voice was too quiet, strained. 'She's missing.'

It was as if Rafe had broken through ice on Lake Morenburg and plunged into the frozen waters beneath. There wasn't enough air in the room. He couldn't fight his way through it. He gripped the sideboard to steady himself. Took some slow breaths.

'How the hell do you lose the *Queen*?'

Steadily the shock morphed into a trickle of fear. She'd said once before she'd walk away. If she'd left, it would serve them all right, especially him since there'd been no one there to protect her from the cruel lies she whispered to herself.

'Have you tried her phone?'

'It's turned off.'

She didn't want to be found. He strode to the window. Looked out at the winding thread of road leading down the mountain to a tiny village that lay a few miles below. A car trundled along, sunlight glinting from the windscreen. Travelling towards the church whose spire he glimpsed, nestled in the valley. The church his parents had married in, where Carl was buried, where he'd been christened. Where life was going on. How could that be when here it felt as if time had screeched to a terrifying halt?

The edges of the phone cut into his hand. He loosened his grasp. 'I'm coming.'

Rafe checked his watch. If his helicopter hadn't been out of commission for servicing, he could have called his pilot to collect him. Driving, he could be back at the palace in an hour, although it might take longer. The car he'd been watching slowed as a herd of cows meandered across the road, then stopped. He ran his hand through his hair. If they didn't want to move, they could block the only road's exit for some time, and he didn't have a four-wheel drive to traverse cross-country.

'There's nothing you can do if palace security has had no success.' Hasselbeck's voice was terse and sharp.

If those words were meant as criticism, he deserved it. It was no worse than the self-flagellation he'd mete out to himself, until Lise was found safe. Time to end this call and go. Outside the little car had managed to get through the roadblock of cows. 'I'll be there in…' It disappeared around a bend and reappeared, closer. Tourists no doubt. This was a popular time of the year in the mountains after all.

Yet the vehicle didn't take the well-worn path, it turned into the road that led to this place. His home.

'Here,' he murmured to himself. Through the trees there was a flicker of movement as the car travelled closer and closer. A tiny flare of hope lit inside. It couldn't be anyone else. Could it? The car pulled to a jerking halt at the front of the house. Its door opened.

Lise. Her golden hair gleaming in the soft light. She glanced up at him and the memory of her coming out ball came rushing back. When she'd looked at him standing at the top of the stairs, with a gentle smile that speared the heart of him sure as Cupid's arrow. He'd wanted to possess her then. Now…

'What?' Sharp frustration in Hasselbeck's voice brought Rafe to his senses.

'Her Majesty's arrived.'

The sigh of abject relief filled his ear. 'I'll send Security.'

'You will listen, Hasselbeck. No security. She's safe with me.' Safer than in a palace full of enemies. Enemies whose job security would be addressed, once he'd repaired the damage he'd done to her on his own. 'I'll bring her back when she's ready.'

Not before. He hung up, tossed the phone on the couch, and took the stairs to the lower level two at a time. If she was never ready to return?

So be it. He would take her wherever she wished to go.

Lise placed her hand on the door handle. It wasn't locked as she turned it, so she pushed the door open and walked inside. Rafe stood in the entrance. Hair an unruly mess of black curls. Delicious stubble grazing his jaw. Dressed in low-slung jeans, a dark T-shirt gripping his muscular body, no shoes. Her legs weakened as he towered in the space. Was his gaze heated as his brown eyes fixed on her? It was hard to tell as she wasn't sure right now what was reality and what was wishful thinking.

'Lise.' Her name came out as a whisper, like a benediction on his lips.

'You were on the phone,' she said. He stood back as she moved further into the hall, shutting the door gently behind her. 'My absence has been noticed?'

'You've aged the prime minister a hundred years.'

'They'll regret having a queen to serve.'

He shook his head. '*Never*. They should be praising the heavens.'

She wanted to rush forward into his arms, beg him to love her, but she held back, as did he. His hands by his sides, fists clenched.

'How did you get a car?' he asked.

For now, a polite conversation was enough. At least they were talking again, without recrimination.

'I sneaked into the palace garages and took one,' she said, and couldn't help a grin of pride. His eyes widened, and then the corner of his own perfect mouth tilted.

'I didn't know that sneaking was in the repertoire of a queen.'

'You'd be surprised what queens can do if they put their minds to it.'

'One thing I've never done is underestimate your abilities.'

He'd always had so much faith in her, even when she'd had none in herself. She dropped her head, scuffing at the floor with her dainty shoe.

'I wanted to find you. There are things I need to say.' She looked up again and he took a step towards her. 'Apologies to make.'

He shook his head, reaching out then hesitating. Running a hand through his hair instead. 'No. There's so much I should have said to you, but I didn't want to add to your pain when I believed you'd had enough. That wasn't my choice to make, especially when you demanded more. I should have remembered you were stronger than anyone realised. Than *you* realise.'

She shrugged. 'You wanted the Crown. I'm not so naïve as to ignore its allure.'

'To my shame, I craved the power over everyone who believed I was less, believing it would somehow make me better. I was wrong.'

'If you're shamed, I am too. I hurt you. I'm no better than those aristocrats at your school who disparaged you, bullied Carl. For that, I'm sorry.' Lise worried at her bottom lip, hoping her apology would be enough. 'The things I said were cruel.'

'They were true.'

She looked at him, standing strong and proud. He had every right to be, given all that he'd achieved.

'You're no farm boy.'

'I am. I've embraced my heritage.' Rafe held out his arms to the sides. 'That's who stands before you. A man, not a king. I should have believed that I was worthy of you. Instead, I was a coward. Afraid of giving you the power to hurt me like no other could, because you alone have that power, Lise.'

She stepped forward, close enough to see the pulse beating strong and sure at the base of his throat. The warmth of his body seeped into hers. The scent of him, like the fresh mountain air that reminded her of freedom.

'As you have the power to hurt me. Because love, when combined with fear, has the power to wound as much as it does to heal. You claimed I could rewrite the fairy tale. I want it. I *deserve* it. To be loved by the man I married. You deserve it too.'

Rafe's mouth opened. Closed. His throat convulsed in a swallow.

'I've protected my heart for a long time.' His voice sounded raw, pained. 'And you were prepared to renounce your claim on the Crown to avoid our marriage.'

She placed her hand over her heart, which thudded in her chest. 'All I wanted was a choice.'

His gaze dropped to the wedding ring that sat on her finger; he cocked his head, the question on his face obvious.

'It's what I wanted for you too. What I asked your father for. A *chance* to offer myself.'

Love filled her, brimming inside. She hoped that what she would say next was enough. It was like standing at the top of a mountain, a steep, snowy slope laid out before her. The thrilling race of her heart in the moments before she pushed off and let herself fly, trusting it would be the perfect run.

'I've spent a lifetime believing that no one truly loved me and yet here I am, standing before you, offering myself to you. Lise Betencourt, woman and Queen.'

Rafe shut his eyes and dropped his head. His shoulders rose and fell before he seemed to gather himself and look at her once more, with a heated gaze piercing into the soul of her.

'In that time we spent together, Lise, when you whispered to me your hopes and dreams for your future, I recognised the incredible woman that you *are*. Now all that I want is a chance to prove myself worthy of you.'

That was when she truly saw it, blazing in his eyes. Naked longing. A softness, she realised now, that was reserved only for her. It was like look-ing in a mirror, because what she saw in Rafe reflected deep inside herself. A need that would never be sated.

Her perfect match. Her other half. Stepping to-wards her with his heart as open as her own.

'Rafe, you were always worthy of me.'

Those words were like a balm to his soul. What a fool he'd been, thinking love wasn't for him. He'd been halfway there before he'd realised how much Lise meant to him, then wondered how the journey had started. He'd hurt her when the simple words *I love you* would have given Lise immu-nity from her fears that others played upon. Her insecurity all caused by him, because he'd been afraid to tell her the extent of feelings he'd refused to acknowledge, in case she rejected him. After all that, self-protection still hadn't saved him. It had only hurt Lise more and that was his deepest regret. The one that almost cleaved him in two and left his heart bruised and bleeding.

'I'll gratefully accept your love as the priceless gift it is, then try to return it a thousandfold. I've done a terrible job of showing you how I feel. I should have protected you and all I did was to hurt you more.'

'We're both good at hurting each other. Do you think we'll be as good at loving each other?'

'I don't accept failure willingly, Lise. I do everything I can to avoid it. In this, I *won't* fail because loving you is easy.'

'You were all I ever wanted. All I still want,' she said. 'Despite our rocky beginning I find I'm still a romantic who believes in happy endings.'

He laughed, the first moment of happiness in these blighted few days. 'I want to hold you now, to prove this is real.'

They fell into each other. Rafe reaching his arms round her, drawing her to his body. She nestled against his strong chest as a voice inside whispered, *She's mine, she's home.* But Lise deserved more.

'Sadly our engagement lacked any romance. It's not like I'd planned.'

'You had a plan?' She pulled back a little, eyebrows raised. 'If I were an ordinary woman, how would you have proposed?'

He pressed his lips to her hair, inhaled the scent of her. Wildflowers, a reminder of spring. Rebirth and renewal.

'The same way as if you were Princess or Queen. Because the royal and the woman are one and the same. I would have brought you here. Into the mountains. To my real home.'

She shook her head. 'My father would never have agreed.'

He couldn't help the wicked smile that broke

free. He dropped his mouth to her ear, so that his breath would caress her throat. 'I could have plucked you from the palace gardens in my helicopter.'

His hand stroked up and down her spine. 'I'd have stolen you from them.'

'A jailbreak.' She shivered. He didn't believe it was from the cold. 'Sounds thrilling.'

'Then I'd get on my knees.' He dropped to the floor in front of her. Took her hands in his. Her fingers were warm against his own, 'And say... Lise, you are my heart, my soul...'

Lise smiled and he was struck silent for a second. He could bask in that look of joy for ever.

'My beginning, my end,' she said.

'You know.' He kissed the ring on her finger, such a precious symbol of all that lay ahead for them. 'The daisy and the rose. These flowers have a meaning. True love. Love at first sight. What a fool I was not to realise, when I married you.'

'I only discovered the secrets of the ring today. And I began to hope. To find the courage to fight for what I wanted.' Tears welled in her eyes then, dripping to her cheeks. Her sadness had felled him. At least these were tears of happiness.

'What would you have said next?' she asked.

He looked into her face, this brave, beautiful woman. Offering her the truth of his love. 'Will you marry a humble farm boy?'

She looked down at him, deep into his eyes. He was once again lost to everything bar the heat of her gaze. 'Yes. I'd be proud to marry him. In fact, if I wasn't married to him already, I'd marry him again.'

'Perhaps we can, in the little church in the valley.'

'Where your parents married?'

He nodded. 'And where Carl is buried. A ceremony for us alone.'

Rafe stood and wrapped her in his arms once more. She melted into his embrace.

'I'd love that,' she said, voice muffled against his chest. 'So, what now?'

He released his hold on her a little. Stroked his palms over her hair and then cupped her face in his hands.

'We live happily ever after.'

'As simple as that?' She smiled and it was like sunrise over the mountain tops, blazing and bright.

Rafe smiled too; he couldn't help himself. 'It's what always happens at the end of a love story.'

She sighed. 'I suppose we should get started on an heir.'

The thought of making love to her again coursed through him like a shot of schnapps. Fiery and intoxicating. But she deserved more, she deserved *everything*.

'I thought you wanted the monarchy to end with you.'

She shrugged. 'I've come to realise the good it can do, that *we* can do. I find I'm not so keen to destroy centuries of my family history out of fear of failure. With you by my side I feel capable of anything.'

He stroked his thumbs over her cheeks, soft and warm under his fingertips.

'*Never* again will you be placed under pressure to perform your role,' he said, his voice firm. 'That includes children. We have a constitution to change first, so there's plenty of time. I have more important things to think about.'

'More important than the country and the Crown?' she asked.

'Yes.' Rafe dropped his head, till his mouth was a mere breath away from hers. 'I have my wife to kiss and there's *nothing* in the world more important than loving her.'

EPILOGUE

Two years later

THE LIGHTS WERE low in their suite as Lise sat gazing into the blissfully sleeping face of Lauritania's newest, three-month-old Princess. Named after the country's longest-serving Queen, their little girl, Marie, had arrived in a squalling rush a month early, but tiny and perfect. Lise cradled her close. Dark lashes brushing delicate pink cheeks. Love overflowed in Lise's heart, a well of feeling that threatened to overcome her as she nestled Marie safe in her arms. The love she and Rafe shared had seemed miraculous enough. She had never imagined she could contain more of the emotion. Their baby proved her wrong.

They had made all kinds of promises when they'd renewed their vows, in a private ceremony. Just the priest and each other, in the little village church. Vows to love, to honour, and then a silent promise that there would be no children until the country's constitution had changed. Rafe stood by their decision, never questioning it until she did. In the end, Lise was tired of others guiding her actions. Because what she and Rafe shared made her strong. She trusted herself, confident she could guide Lauritania through the coming years ahead. Rafe's love had given that to her. As a team, they were *invincible*. Nothing was impossible with her husband by her side. He believed in her, and she believed in herself. Marie was proof of that. Their daughter planned, wanted, adored. All of it achieved through love. Passionate. Unassailable. Eternal.

As if she'd conjured him, Rafe walked into the room, devastatingly handsome and still in a suit despite the late hour. Campaigning to the last, no doubt, for the most important vote of their lives. He stopped as he took them in. Mother and daughter. His lips curved into a tender smile.

'Now there's a perfect scene. My two beloveds.'

He came to her and stroked his hand through her hair. She tilted her head to him. He bowed down and brushed his lips over hers, the thrill at his touch as fresh and intoxicating as the first time. Rafe then moved to drop a gentle kiss on their baby's head. The little girl stirred, took a deep breath, and sighed before nestling into Lise once more.

'No word?' she whispered, almost not daring to hope.

He shook his head. 'Not yet.'

'If we fail today, we'll keep trying until we succeed.'

Even though change came slowly to Lauritania, the constitutional debate and vote seemed to be going later into the night than she'd expected. But she would never give up on this. Marie was destined to be Lauritania's next Queen. And she *would* rule the country on her own terms, without the need to marry. Lise's speech to support constitutional change had been a statement of fact and intent, of how lucky *she* had been in love, for sure, but promoting a fervent desire to give their firstborn choices without limitation. Rafe's campaign had been no less forceful, with all the passion of the protector he was.

'Your people adore you. Adore our daughter,' Rafe murmured. 'When have we ever failed?'

There was only truth in his words. Success had mounted on success. The country's economy turning around. After Hasselbeck had lost the support of Parliament, they had a new prime minister who worked with his Queen rather than against her. Lauritanians were ecstatic at the young, vibrant royal family leading the country to a grand renewal. Now, every day was filled with happiness and hope. Yet their work was not yet complete.

'I want *everything* for our child.'

'And she'll have it because she has us. Does she need to be put down?'

Lise looked down at the baby's peaceful, sleeping face once more. 'Yes. But it's hard to let her go.'

'I know.' Rafe held out his hands, raised an eyebrow. Lise smiled as she relinquished Marie to him. He gently took his swaddled babe into his arms, an unfailing cocoon of safety he provided to their child and to her. She stood and Rafe watched, his gaze turning molten as she stretched. He'd worshipped her through every phase of her pregnancy. The morning sickness, her rampant hormones with their crying jags, in the aftermath of her fast and furious labour. And now, the ample curves of new motherhood.

'As beautiful as your mama,' he whispered into their daughter's dark shock of curls, just like his own.

'More like her father.'

He grinned, and it lit a fire of joy inside her to see her two most beloved like this. 'Heaven help us all.'

'If she's like her father her country should call itself lucky to have her.' And they did. The people adored Rafe too, the man who was their King. Praised his brilliance at helping guide the economy into recovery. His love and care for the country and their Queen.

He gently placed Marie into her bassinet, then held out his arms. Lise walked into his embrace as he brushed his lips against hers once more and then deepened the kiss. She threaded her fingers into his hair. The emotion flowing between them, through them, like a bright and living flame.

A knock sounded at the door and her heart rate spiked. Rafe broke the kiss and rested his forehead on hers, his breath gusting over her lips. 'It will all be well. How can't it be when we have each other?'

She drifted her thumb across his lips, and he kissed its tip.

'Come in,' she said and turned as the door opened to Albert. Rafe squeezed her hip in support, and she swallowed but didn't move away. Their physical affection as strong for each other in public as it was in private. A mark of their reign. They stood together as one on this as they did on everything. Albert beamed at them both.

'The vote was unanimous. No dissenters. Congratulations, Your Majesties, and to Her Littlest Highness. The constitution is changed.'

Lise shut her eyes against the fresh sting of tears as Rafe gave his thanks for the news and Albert took his leave. She opened her eyes to flashes outside. Then the boom and crack as fireworks burst out all over the city. She and Rafe went to the window and flung it wide to the drifting sound of cheers rising across the capital.

All for them and the little girl who was Lauritania's distant future.

'I had no idea they'd be so happy,' she said, wiping at the tears slipping down her cheeks.

'They are because they love you. Though never as much as I do,' he said, his voice rough and raw. 'And for this moment, I have a gift.'

Rafe reached into his pocket and pulled out a ring.

'What's this?' she whispered, as an oval yellow diamond twinkled in the low lights of the room.

'You said you didn't need anything for our engagement, but this is more. An eternity ring.' He slipped it onto her finger, then took her trembling hands in his own sure grip. 'You are the sunshine of my life. A source of endless happiness. I hope this ring will remind you that I love you more each passing day. That you were destined to be my for ever, from the moment I set eyes on you.'

Lise looked up at him, this man she adored beyond reason. Good and kind and honest…and *hers*.

'I never need a reminder because that certainty is here.' She placed her hand in the middle of her chest. 'I hold your love in my heart, where it's always with me. Always safe. No one can ever take that away.'

As the capital continued to celebrate, the sky lit in showers of rainbow sparks around them, Lise slid her arms round Rafe's neck.

'I look forward to my for ever with you,' she whispered. 'There's nowhere I'd rather be.'

He smiled at her, soft and warm. Eyes alight and burning with adoration, mirroring what she carried for him, within herself. Then he dropped his head to hers and murmured against her lips, 'Let me show you eternity, my love.'

* * * * *

If you couldn't get enough of
The Marriage That Made Her Queen
then the next instalments in the
Behind the Palace Doors… trilogy
will blow you away!

Also, don't miss out on these other
Kali Anthony stories!

Revelations of His Runaway Bride
Bound as His Business Deal Bride
Off-Limits to the Crown Prince
Snowbound in His Billion-Dollar Bed

Available now!